BLOOD DEBT

EL MUNDO DE SANGRE

DIAMANTE DE SANGRE
BOOK TWO

LANA SKY

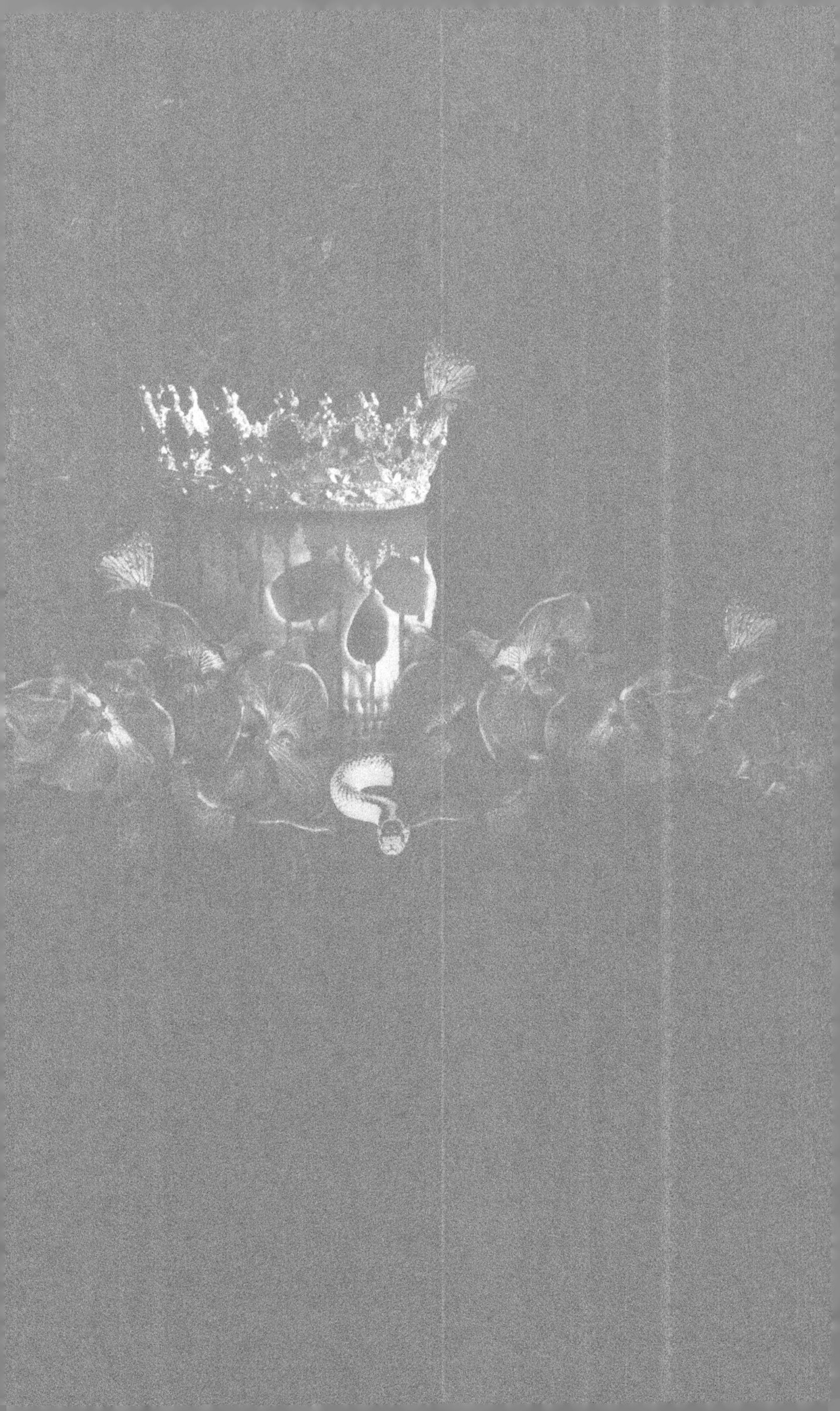

Blood Debt

Blood Debt By Lana Sky

Copyright © 2023 by Lana Sky
All rights reserved.

No part of this publication may be reproduced, distributed, or transmitted in any form or by any means, including photocopying, recording, or other electronic or mechanical methods, without the prior written permission of the author.

This is a work of fiction. Names, characters, businesses, places, events and incidents are either the products of the author's imagination or used in a fictitious manner. Any resemblance to actual persons, living or dead, or actual events is purely coincidental.

Cover Design and Interior Formatting by Charity Chimni
Editing and Proofreading by Charity Chimni
Alpha Reading by Jessica Rita Rampersad

ACKNOWLEDGMENTS

Thanks so much to everyone who supported this draft along the way, including the many beta readers who provided encouragement! Please keep in mind that this story includes dark, graphic, and explicit content matter that may not be suitable for readers under the age of 18—or for readers who are uncomfortable with the following subject matter: explicit sex, forcible unwanted touch, mentions of domestic violence, mentions of child abuse, graphic depictions of violence, and mild gore.

I don't experience blissful darkness during my drug-induced sleep. My final moments with Jaguar haunt me like a nightmare. His touch. Our kiss. My confession…

With every passing second, it sinks in that these words weren't a figment of my cruel imagination—I said them out loud. Finally, after days of pretending to be Tiena, I revealed my true identity to him…

I can't believe I made such a stupid and careless mistake. The intent behind lies isn't important to men like Julian Domingas. They crush dishonesty wherever it festers—they have no choice, if they want to maintain their power, that is. In any case, I'll pay dearly for this deception. Half expecting to find myself in his pet jaguar's cage as a punishment, I warily open my eyes.

The room I blink into clarity vaguely resembles the dank chamber I was locked in at Gatita's mercy, and my stomach twists in grim anticipation. Various shades of steel gray paint the walls, evoking iron bars, but in a far more luxurious setting. Instead of a bloody floor, I lie on a bed, surrounded by stark, modern furniture.

A bedroom?—yes, but definitely not Jaguar's. There's a different smell, a different feel to the air from his usual haunt. Not only that... The view beyond the large windows is rugged, with dark shapes on the horizon I can only assume to be mountains, not exactly the typical Texas skyline.

Where am I? Trying to sit upright, I wince. *Shit.* My head is pounding, my muscles aching. Forget this new mind game. It's tempting to curl up beneath the blankets—lush, expensive sheets—and sleep until Jaguar comes.

He's bound to do so anyway, eager to reveal what he has in store. Why waste time worrying?

As if taunting me, male laughter seeps through the windowpane, bringing a new level of fear. Jaguar's—I'd know that rasping voice anywhere—but he isn't alone. His characteristic chuckle is immediately followed by a softer, higher-pitched laugh.

It's a child's.

No... Soreness forgotten, I struggle from beneath the bedsheets and hit the floor on my hands and knees. A groan rips from me as I attempt to stand. I have to throw myself at the window, blinking to bring the world into focus. It is obvious from the view that we are not in Jaguar's Texas villa with Italian-style architecture. Featuring sleek lines and concrete-colored walls, this home is a modern masterpiece.

Although I've never been here before, the layout seems familiar. How?

That mystery can wait. My heart races as I see a tall man standing at the center of a square terrace below. Even without the cocky posture he displays for his posse, that hulking form is unmistakable. Jaguar. Instead of preening bimbos, his attention is devoted to his sole companion struggling to dribble a basketball beside him. *Oh, God.* That figure's tiny, familiar proportions make me cry out.

"Franco!"

I whirl from the window and hit the floor hard. Gritting my teeth, I crawl toward a partially-open door across from the bed. The exit? It seems so. Sweat drips down my neck as I push past it and peer into a spacious hallway. Gray walls, bathed in sunlight, create a mocking contrast to my new reality. This is no sanctuary but a prison.

And I'm in no state to fight. My knees buckle as I cling to the nearest wall and haul myself upright. I'm so unsteady as I stagger from the room, that I collide with someone standing nearby. Their grip on my forearm keeps me from collapsing again, and I crane my neck to take in my captor fully. A man, with gruff features and cold, dark eyes. Belatedly, his name comes to me—*Horatio,* Jaguar's righthand man.

Will he drag me back to bed on his master's orders? No. With a terse nod, he steps aside, gesturing with a wave of his hand. "This way," he mutters before marching ahead. I follow him through a winding corridor decorated with abstract paintings that resemble shadows and bloodstains thrown over beige canvases. Trying to keep up, I pant as the rest of the house passes by in a blur until we reach the sliding glass doors on the lower level, where the outdoor space is visible.

"Let me out!" A rush of adrenaline surges through me, and I lunge, eager to bolt through the glass if I have to, but Horatio opens both doors without comment.

As I rush onto the stone terrace barefoot, I barely notice the man who steps forward to greet me. "It's about time you joined us, Lupe—"

"Franco!" I push past Jaguar without a second thought. The danger I'm in doesn't even matter. I only have eyes for this beautiful little boy with a cherub grin behind him. God, it's really him. As I cry his name again, he drops his ball and runs to me.

"Auntie!"

"Oh, Francisco!" I wrap him in my arms and squeeze so tight he squeals in protest.

As I frantically kiss his cheek, he cries out, "Too tight, Auntie—"

"It seems your mother is awake, Francisco." *Damn.*

That blunt tone acts like a bucket of ice water thrown over my head. My arms go limp, allowing Franco to wiggle free. I can't even face the man looming over me. Instead, I just watch his shadow, a formless black entity stretching across the pavement to swallow me whole.

"It's good to see you on your feet, Tiena," he continues. "How relieved you must feel to be reunited with your...*son*. What a difficult time you've had worrying about him."

Even though I feel his eyes on me, I ignore him, focusing only on Franco. It's impossible to stop touching his face and smoothing the glossy black hair from his round cheeks. The moment I'm sure he's not a figment of my exhaustion, I ask my most pressing question. "Are you okay, honey?"

Nodding, he opens his mouth to speak, but a deeper voice overrides him. "What a marvelous coincidence that you would awaken *now*."

Silence falls, allowing me a few dangerous seconds to replay his words. *Mother*, not Aunt. Although my final memories of my time in his bed are fuzzy, one remains clear—dazed, drugged, and exhausted out of my skull, I told him who I was—I am certain of it.

Had he heard me? I don't know if now is a good time to come clean, with Franco finally in my sights. I can see the confusion in my sweet boy's eyes, and I force a smile, desperate to placate him.

"You're safe now, baby," I murmur, kissing his cheek again. "I've missed you so, so much."

It would be so nice if my love alone could teleport us away from the man who stares down at us with an unmistakable smile. When I finally glance Jaguar's way, his chilling expression reveals why he planned this dramatic reunion in the first place—to open my eyes to the truth.

He owns us.

Yet… Despite his dangerous aura, I'd almost forgotten how handsome he is. His eyes gleam in the waning daylight, his skin kissed gold by the sunset. His muscular body is accentuated by a black shirt that clings to every inch of his chest. Even as I feel my skin crawl with fear at his nearness, my belly flips. The thin material draped over my body feels as effective as tissue paper against him.

With one look, he strips me naked. Vulnerable. Exposed.

"Franco, I'll let you and your mama chat," he says with a gallant grin, snapping me back to awareness. Amusement never reaches those glittering eyes, however. These are sharp, heavy-lidded, and full of mystery. God, what does he remember? "Relax, Tiena," he scolds as if reading my mind, "you and your boy will have the run of the house. I can promise that you won't be disturbed. Then we can discuss what you missed while you were out."

"You were sleeping for a long time," Franco pitches in. "The whole day!"

"I'm sure you both are exhausted, Franco," Jaguar chides, but his grin never falters. "Later on, we can play that video game again. If you think you can beat me, you are sorely mistaken."

"Okay!" Franco perks up, his eyes glittering with excitement as he tracks Jaguar's retreat. It's an expression I don't recognize in him. He didn't look at Braulio like that.

Then again, Braulio never paid him any mind unless it was to beat him into submission.

God, what have I gotten us into?

"Can I go with him now?" he asks me, craning his neck in the direction Jaguar went off in. "Please?"

"Just… Slow down, baby. Let me look at you." I stroke my fingers through his hair and then cup his beautiful face against my palm. It hurts to see how much he resembles Tiena. She always had that Cheshire-cat grin. Is she still smirking now, unconcerned about the welfare of her own son? Even if she is, that isn't my problem. Meeting Franco's gaze, I force myself to smile back. "Are you okay, sweetheart?"

He looks cleaner in an orange shirt and shorts than he ever did on Braulio's estate. Still, I can't trust his happiness is entirely genuine—even though his hair is neatly combed, his face is clean, and his beautiful grin is on full display. Jaguar is incapable of entertaining a woman without threatening her life every five minutes. No way could he properly safeguard a child.

It doesn't matter that Franco's smiling. Actually smiling. Until he catches me staring and wrinkles his nose.

"Auntie, what's wrong? And why did he call you my mama's name? Where is she?" He looks around, scanning for her in the shadows.

"Franco…" I drag him into my arms and place my mouth near his ear, praying he understands how much I love him.

How sorry I am. "I don't know, but I'm looking for her. I swear I am, baby. But for now, I need you to pretend for me, okay. Call me Mama. Just think of it as a game. I know you're confused. And Jaguar... Mr. Domingas. Stay away from him. He is a very busy man. How long have you been here with him?"

"Today. The morning, I think." Franco shrugs, scrunching his nose as he tries to remember. "I came by airplane—"

"Did he talk to you?" I prod. "Mr. Domingas?"

"Yeah. He was there when the plane landed. He said he's Papa's friend. Can I go play with him now? He's fun."

"No," I snap. Then I remember the ruse I signed up for— the eager mistress to a dangerous psychopath, all in the name of protecting my so-called son. With Franco within his reach as a token to control me, I cannot risk upsetting Jaguar now. Not yet, anyway. "I-I mean... Sure, but can I watch?"

"Yeah! Let's go. This way!" Grinning, he takes my hand, pulling me along.

While I slept, it seems he explored the house thoroughly. With cheerful narration, he gives me a guided tour of our route to meet Jaguar.

"That's the living room. It has a big TV on the wall! And there's a really big kitchen over there."

He points his finger as he speaks and, as I swivel my head to take in every new feature, I slowly begin to understand why this place felt so familiar before. It wasn't for nothing that

Jaguar presented me with real estate listings—I chose this house out of the three he suggested. The elegant modern mansion composed of concrete and glass.

I must admit that it is more beautiful in person. The design choices are minimal compared to the previous mansion, but Jaguar's primal allure somehow fits this setting better. The black and gray color scheme enhances his mystique—not to mention that concrete is easier to clean blood off of than white marble and fancy wallpaper.

With that grim imagery in mind, I can only dread what his "game room" might look like.

"The basement is this way," Franco explains as we near a winding staircase leading to a finished lower level sporting several rooms. In one of them, Jaguar sits in a leather recliner positioned before a massive flat-screen television. An array of various video games line shelves along the walls, spanning every recent decade, it seems.

"It's about time," Jaguar says with a wink in Franco's direction. "Ready to lose?" He has a gaming remote in one hand and tosses one to Franco as we enter.

"Not on your life!" Eagerly, Franco climbs onto a recliner beside him, and they commence with a loud, violent round of whatever game they've chosen to play.

At the back of the room, I watch them, ready to jump in at a moment's notice. If Jaguar speaks at him too loudly. Looks at him wrong. Anything—I'll step in, no matter the risk. With each passing minute, I'm reduced to a sweating, twitching mess, unable to move...

Because the cruel, vicious narco never gives me a reason to.

That's the scary part. With the boy, he displays more restraint than Braulio ever did. That bastard would snap at Franco. Tease him in the next breath. Casually threaten him with a beating if the urge struck him.

Then he'd buy him a toy to make up for it.

Jaguar is different. It's clear that he listens to him, sincerely listens. When Franco gets too competitive and threatens to throw his controller, Jaguar gently reels him in. No matter the outburst, the man never raises his voice once. Instead, he coaches Franco with a gentle authority I almost admire.

"Patience, son," he insists after a particularly brutal defeat. "Losing isn't what diminishes you. It's not learning a damn thing from it. Watch me. It only takes one win to turn the tables."

God, trembling in a delicate nightgown, I've never hated this man like I do now. I've never feared him so much. Brutality from him, I could understand—or if he callously ignored Franco or tried to use him for leverage right from the start. I'd almost prefer that to this show of kindness, because I know it's an act. Sooner or later, he'll hurt us both.

But he won't get the chance. As I endure these torturous moments with a blank expression, I develop a plan. I'll wait until sundown and steal Franco away with no one the wiser. We'll run off into the night, and I'll contact Pedro for assistance somehow. Yes, it's a good plan—that, or my senses are still dulled enough from whatever drug made me sleep this long that I'm blinded to the idiocy.

No matter. It's all I've got.

"Congrats, my friend! You've handily won that round," Jaguar bellows, making me startle back to the present. After patting Franco on the shoulder, he rises to shut off the machine. "Franco, my friend Horatio got you something to eat—"

"You're not coming?" Franco turns to me, frowning in a way that makes me ache to run to him.

I've barely taken a step when Jaguar raises his hand. "Of course, she will," he assures the boy. "But I need to talk to your mama alone first."

"Wait!" I take another step, breaking his silent command. "So soon? We've barely had any time to—"

"Later, Tiena," Jaguar says with a dismissive laugh. "Let the boy eat. You can smother him in a bit, *sí*? Go fill your belly, Francisco. I'll return your mama to you soon enough. I told Horatio to get you chicken tenders and fries. You like that?"

"Yeah!" Oblivious to my terror, Franco happily skips off.

Five brutal seconds pass in silence—just enough time for Franco to leave earshot. The second he does, Jaguar whirls on me with a lethal grace. His hand shoots out, and his thumb hooks beneath the collar of my nightgown, tugging me toward him.

"Few things will piss me off, Tiena, but do you want to know what will?" His eyes cut to slits. "You looking at me like you're waiting for me to devour your son in one bite." Within seconds, he has me close enough to wrap his hand around my throat, but nowhere near hard enough to choke. "Locking you in a cage with my precious kitty is one thing, but I will never harm him. Do you understand? Not to get to you, or even Braulio. I have other methods to hurt you. *Claro*? Say it."

I fight for air. "I-I believe you—"

"No." He squeezes a fraction harder. "Say that you know in your soul that I will never lay a hand on him. Say it."

"I… I can't." I bat his hand away, but to my surprise…

He lets me go.

With all the strength I can muster, I lift my chin and hold his probing stare unflinchingly. "What kind of mother would I be if I just took your word for it?" I demand, co-opting his use of the word. "Even his own father…"

No. He doesn't need to know the extent of the abuse. Then he could threaten to send Franco back when it suits him.

Teeth gritted, I try a different tact. "I need to see I can trust you with him. Until then, I won't. You can command my body, but you can't command my trust, not in this instance."

"Is that so?" Jaguar asks with flashing eyes. "Yet you came crawling to me for help. *Unless* you weren't entirely honest before—" A smile shapes his lips rather than a frown. The contradiction amuses him. "Don't tell me your plans have changed, Lupe? Especially now that I went through all the trouble of finding your...*son*. Let's not be ungrateful now, *sí*? A good *mother* won't change her mind so quickly. She wouldn't do a damn thing that could put the boy in any danger. For example—" He's on me before I can blink, hooking his hand around my neck to draw me close. Forcing eye contact, I feel the nail of his thumb tease the flesh above my pulse point. "She wouldn't use him as a shield to save her own skin, now, would she?"

The blood drains from my face as he releases me so abruptly, I sway, suddenly lightheaded. If I had any doubts about whether he heard my confession, the truth is confirmed now—he knows.

"Oh yes." As if reading my mind, he nods, his teeth bared. "You see now, don't you, *Lupita*?"

All I can do is try to explain. "Jaguar, I—"

"Don't change your tact now," he snaps back, his tone cold. It's as if a haunting gleam creeps into his eyes, making them appear ten times darker. Fathomless. "No excuses. No convincing explanations, either. You came to me under the pretense of a desperate *mother* who claimed she would do anything for our poor Francisco. I would hate to learn that your devotion was a lie. So, tell me, Lupe, will you continue to fight for him, or was he only ever a useful tool?"

"Jaguar..." I'm gaping at him, my mouth open. A tool. What the hell is that supposed to mean? With Franco's safety on the line, I'd be a fool to challenge him. Yet, I can't stop myself.

"Is that a threat?" I croak.

He doesn't say anything. His stern expression suggests he wants me to agonize over that question. One thing becomes evident as his jaw clenches with anger—this isn't just about a mistaken identity.

Something else has him simmering, seconds from lashing out.

"Of course not." Suddenly, he smiles, but it's a feral display of teeth without an ounce of warmth to be found. "A threat would imply I wasn't serious, but I've gotten to know Franco while you were napping the day away. He is a good boy. I would hate to see that his welfare has been used as a ploy to pull on my heartstrings."

He fingers a piece of my hair while I stand there, paralyzed. *A ploy?*

"I don't..." I stammer to find the right words. "I don't understand what's wrong—"

"Don't you?" With that smirk still on his face, he releases me and turns toward the door. "I don't appreciate having my generosity taken advantage of, or watching those in my orbit use *pawns* in an attempt to manipulate me. While you may not be his mother, your duty to Franco remains clear. You either care for the boy, or you don't—" His tone hardens as he tilts his head to shoot me a piercing glance. "Don't flip the script now. *Claro?*"

My poor, exhausted brain rushes to try and decipher what lurks between the lines of his words. *Prove my devotion to Franco wasn't a lie—that I'm not using him for my own gain?*

"Come up and join us for dinner," he says, giving me whiplash at the sudden change of subject. "I made sure to order his favorite. If you're lucky, he'll leave some scraps for you. Ciao, for now, Lupe." With that, Jaguar strolls from the room, whistling a chilling, jaunty tune that echoes in his wake. The second I hear his steps on the staircase, I collapse to my knees, gasping for air.

Oh, God. My eyes burn as I try to fight back the tears. What am I going to do?

Focus, for one, I decide with a firm shake of my head. Get my bearings. Not panic. And certainly not leave Franco unattended in the home of an infamous narco. Providing Jaguar still aims to keep Franco safe, then I will go along with whatever he wants, no matter what the game is— though I wonder why he cares? Anger at being lied to, I could understand, but this seems to go deeper. The look in his eye when he demanded I be clear about my intentions toward Franco... It wasn't cold, or calculating, but protective. As if he genuinely thinks I sought to use the boy merely to get to him.

My mind wanders before I can help myself, probing deeper into the prospect. Perhaps, as a boy, was Jaguar used by his own mother?

Enough, Pita, I tell myself with a firm shake of my head. *Snap out of it. Focus on Franco. Only on Franco.*

Bracing myself against the wall for balance, I stand and then make my way from the room, straining my ears for Franco's voice. Eventually, I find myself in a spacious dining room dominated by a long, glass table. At one end, Franco sits, dunking chicken fingers into his own private array of sauces.

I savor a few seconds of watching him from the shelter of the doorway. My poor little Franco. He seems so big, after only a few weeks. His baby fat is starting to melt away, revealing the handsome bone structure beneath. In a few years, he'll resemble his mother even more, and the thought hurts like hell. Does Tiena, wherever she is, even miss him?

"Au—Mama!" Spotting me, Franco grins and then wrinkles his nose. With a ketchup-smeared finger, he points at my legs. "Why are you wearing that thing? Is it a costume?"

"Huh?" I ask, inspecting my outfit for the first time. The ivory, lacy shift that swishes around my legs with every step is, thankfully, way more modest than one of Jaguar's risqué choices for me regarding clothing. In fact, the cut resembles something a nun might wear, hence Franco's assumption.

In contrast, the man who strokes his chin as I approach represents nothing holy.

"Your mama was in such a rush to meet you here that she forgot her clothes," Jaguar says from his perch at the head of the table. From my previous position, I hadn't been able to see him. "We shall have to take her shopping, yes?"

I assume it's a boast, given that he has his women share clothing between them like living barbie dolls. Still, I force a smile.

"I'll let you pick my clothing, baby, if you want. What would you like me to wear?"

"Pink!" He grins before chomping on a ketchup-soaked nugget.

"Pink?" Jaguar laughs and takes his time inspecting me from head to toe. Deviously, he lets his gaze linger over my breasts before finally meeting my gaze. "I don't know if I can see it. Your mama seems the opposite of soft and sweet. Perhaps red suits her better. The color of blood."

I flinch at the way his teeth catch over the supposed "compliment."

"Not uh. Pink," Franco says playfully. I'm sure the darker innuendo has gone right over his head. "But she doesn't like dresses. She likes pants."

"Oh, is that so?" Jaguar raises an eyebrow and traces his bottom lip with his tongue. It's a shameless display, put on just beyond Franco's line of sight. *Dios mío*, his eyes *devour* me through the thin material. "Pants, you say. How do you think she'd look in mine?"

Franco cackles gleefully. "Silly."

"I'm sorry, Francisco." In contrast, Jaguar's laugh is low and guttural. "I think I may have to disagree on that, my son."

"F-Franco," I croak, reaching for his hand. "We shouldn't keep Mr. Domingas. I'm sure he's very busy."

"Your mama is right," Jaguar says, but I know in my gut it's too easy a retreat. Based on the searching look he sends my way, I will pay for this sooner or later. Goosebumps erupt on my skin as he stands, his smile strained but polite. "I'll go to my study and get started on my busy, boring work. Franco, why don't you show your mama to your room when you're done eating? She hasn't had the chance to explore yet."

"Okay! It's so big," Franco says, turning to me, his eyes bright. "My room even has a TV, Au—Mama!"

"I can't wait to see it, honey." I stroke my fingers through his hair, desperate to avoid eye contact with the figure lurking just beyond my field of view.

Yet he won't easily be ignored. "*Lupita*—" his voice catches over the syllables in the name. "When you've tucked him in, come see me. We have unfinished business, you and I."

"Business?" I cough to hide my fear, but his feral smile tells me he knows damn well how unnerved I am.

"Nothing serious," he replies. As if to undercut those words, he lets his tongue slide along his lower lip in a devious display of innuendo. Sweat drips down my back as I rush to interpret the gesture. A threat? "Just… To discuss concerns any parent may have regarding the welfare of their child. *Adíos.*"

Shit. With unparalleled grace, he leaves, though I'm sure one of his minions, like Horatio, is lurking out of sight, ready to ensure his master's wishes are brought to fruition.

Any fantasies I had about escaping die.

Tonight, he won't let me out of his sight.

Perhaps…not *ever.*

CHAPTER TWO

Like a burgeoning storm cloud, Jaguar's departure ushers in a sense of doom. Replaying his parting words in my head, I'm sure there was a threat hidden amongst them somewhere. Were I alone, I'd panic and fret.

But I'm not, and Francisco doesn't deserve to see me cower.

I fake a cheerful demeanor for his sake by forcing a smile. "Eat, baby," I demand, prodding his mostly-full plate. "Tell me what you've been up to. I hope you've been okay."

"I'm fine," he replies in a deadpan tone. His expression turns glum, and his gaze downcast as if Jaguar stole his joy when he left.

"Franco?" The hairs on the back of my neck go up. I know that haunted, vacant expression. For the past decade, I've sported that same look, always fearful, always on guard. "Tell me what happened after you left your papa's house, baby."

My voice is choked with panic and guilt. Jaguar promised me all along that Franco was safe, but what is safety to a narco? Only God knows what the boy witnessed while being taken from his father's home.

I place my hand on his shoulder until he looks up at me. "Please, honey. Tell me what happened."

"It was nighttime," he says in a small voice. "Papa said I had to leave and stay at the California house. He had Chino and Guapo take me—"

"Just those two?" I ask, frowning. They're Braulio's most trusted lieutenants. The bastard wasn't just being petty by moving Franco out of state and away from me. By sending those men to guard his son, he'd been worried for the boy, in his own sick way. Why? I scan his delicate features, desperate for an answer. "Honey, do you know why?"

He shakes his head. "No. Auntie… Are my mama and papa coming today too? Are they here?"

Damn. I sigh and sit back in my chair. How I've been dreading this question. Rather than evade it, I suck in a breath and do the one thing I've been fearing since setting off on this course of action—I tell him some version of the truth. "No, they aren't coming, honey. Franco, I think it's best if your papa stays away for now. He has a lot of stuff on his plate. All that matters is that you are safe—"

"No!" I feel my heart pang as he looks down at his plate and says, "You're lying. He won't come. He's dead, isn't he?"

"N-No, baby." I rush to pat his back. Did Jaguar plant this seed in his head? As much as I loathe Braulio, I can't deny that seeing Franco's heartbroken frown arouses the grim reality I've been trying to ignore all this time. At the end of the day, this child loves his parents, both of them. What happens to them in this twisted narco game will affect him no matter what.

Perhaps, this is the real reason behind Jaguar's taunts? He holds Franco's physical and emotional well-being right in the palm of his hand—and I'm the one who put both there.

"Franco, baby, look at me—" I stroke his hair until he complies. His brown eyes glisten with unshed tears, and I feel my eyes well in response. My poor boy. "Where did you hear that from? Did someone say that to you?"

"No, but I'm not stupid." He sniffles, batting me away. "He *has* to be dead. Papa was afraid, and I heard the men who brought me here talking. They said, 'you know whose kid this is? Braulio, the dead man walking—'" A sob cracks through the stoic demeanor he tries so hard to uphold.

"Oh, Franco." I pull him into my arms, blinking as those menacing tears finally fall. "Your daddy is alive. He just... He just can't be here right now—"

"And my mama?" he demands, pulling back with a questioning grimace. "They just left me here."

"She loves you, baby," I insist, gently wiping his tears, first with my fingers and then with a napkin snatched from the table. "They both do."

It kills me to say that, but I know he needs to hear it.

Suddenly, he grabs my hand. "Auntie. Before I left, I heard Papa say… He said bad things. I'm scared." Fear floods those beautiful brown eyes, and I squeeze his hand, desperate to reassure him.

"Let's not think about that now," I say. "It seems like you're finished eating. Why don't you show me your room?"

"Okay!" He smiles, and any hint of despair vanishes as he bounds up a winding main staircase and into a room down the hall from where I woke up. As he'd excitedly conveyed earlier, it's spacious, painted orange, and decorated perfectly to the tastes of a young boy.

I'm surprised that Jaguar even took the time to do so.

I'm…impressed.

Paranoia supplies a million different potential motives for the gesture—none stemming from the goodness of Jaguar's black heart. A fully decorated room to Franco's particular tastes doesn't seem like a temporary arrangement, and as Franco enters a closet already stocked with clothing in his size, I do a double take. Jaguar didn't mean this to be a brief stay before returning to his manor laden with bimbos.

It seems, he aims to keep us here.

Though hell, if Franco and I both can live in a mansion, far away from him, that can't possibly be a bad thing. Can it?

While Franco chooses an outfit for the night and bathes in a claw-foot tub in his very own en suite, I try not to let my fear show.

Jaguar may be a psychopath, but he does know quality architecture.

His ability to distract traumatized boys is also impressive. This Franco, giggling beneath a layer of bubble bath, doesn't even compare to the quiet, shell of a boy I saw last in Braulio's grasp. He's animated, chattering aimlessly about video games and toys, unconcerned by his sudden change of scenery. He doesn't even bring up his parents as much as I thought, though a new figure seems to dominate nearly every other topic he mentions, "Mr. Jaguar said that—"

"No, baby. *Mr. Domingas,*" I sternly correct, earning a startled glance from Franco. *Damn it.* "I just mean…" I choke out a nervous laugh and run my fingers through his damp hair, hoping I come across as playful. "He is a very powerful man, but he isn't our friend. You just met him, after all. We must be respectful."

"Yeah." Franco nods, scrunching his nose in agreement. "He's nice, though. He played with me while you were sleeping."

I feel the blood drain from my face. "W-What? How?"

I brace myself for mentions of bloodied cages or hungry pet felines.

My terror eases a little when Franco shrugs. "Video games and ball. He showed me how to dribble. I've been wanting to learn forever." His voice grows soft, his eyes downcast. "Papa was always too busy."

From his awed tone, I suspect that Braulio rarely had time for him. Not long ago, I would visit him nearly every day when allowed, but I rarely stayed long. There was only so much of Tiena and her antics that I could take. While there, however, I spent nearly all my time with Franco, and I regret not rescuing him sooner.

Well, I'm here now. I intend to shower him with all the affection I have. After drying him off, I hug him for far too long. He has to tug at my hair before I finally relent and follow him back into his bedroom.

"Goodnight, baby." I squeeze him one last time before tucking him into bed. Then I shut off the lights and prepare to leave.

Only I don't.

Upon waking up to an orange stream of daylight flooding the room hours later, I realize with horror that I slept here, right beside Franco's bed. Still dozing, he is blissfully unaware of my presence. After kissing him on the cheek, I sneak into the hall and wander to my room.

Thank God, Jaguar isn't lurking inside. His absence, however, only fuels my increasing dread of our inevitable meeting. I refuse to sit around waiting for him in a nightgown, though. I search the room and find a door that leads to a large walk-in closet. Before Jaguar forced me to swallow that supposed sleeping pill, I don't remember packing, but I expect him to provide at least a change of clothes.

Instead, I find every shelf bare, every hanger empty. A gasp escapes my lips as I feel my heart sink. Oh, God. Is this his way of telling me that, while he prepared this house for Franco, I'm not welcome? Will he separate us again?

Dios mío, I couldn't bear it. My eyes well up with tears, and I collapse onto the edge of the bed, feeling sick to my stomach. As I'm lost in thought, I don't notice when a shadow falls over the door.

Not until it's too late.

"Finally, the vicious little viper dares to make an appearance," a low, rasping voice calls out. Slowly, I look up at the creature watching me through the doorway.

A monster looms ahead, his eyes dangerously dark, his expression cold. A black shirt and pants accentuate his feral nature, and the resulting look sends shivers down my spine. Remarkably, it doesn't feel like fear.

A strained prickling sensation builds beneath my skin as he cocks his head to take me in with a searching glance that starts with my head and slowly travels downward. Heavy-lidded eyes, dark with raw lust, rake over my trembling limbs with an open hunger he had enough tact not to display in front of Franco.

There's no hiding it now. My throat goes dry as I notice the front of his slacks strain. When his fingers twitch at his sides, I'm sure he'll issue some degrading command. *On your knees...*

Instead, he clenches his jaw so hard a muscle twitches, as if to fight back the desire. Only then do I see the anger smoldering in his gaze. Hell, maybe I imagined the previous lust merely to stall.

For the first time, I'm forced to face the wrath of Julian Domingas with no relief in sight.

"I've humored you, Lupe," he growls, flexing one muscular hand in and out of a fist. When he takes a step, I jump, too stunned to stand. "I've played your little game and endured your haughty little attitude for long enough. But I refuse to allow you to insult me. Not here, on my own damn property. You spin a sweet little tale about needing my help, only to turn your nose up at me like I'm a piece of shit when you get your way. Oh, no, Lupe..." With three long strides, he gains on me, reaching out with his fingers extended. "I will—"

"Thank you," I blurt before he can touch me. It feels important to say it, even if I loathe the pleading note in my voice. While I gaze at him from beneath my lashes, I don't conceal my sincere gratitude. "For keeping Francisco safe. For making him comfortable. Thank you."

He didn't have to. Even I can admit that.

Jaguar stops short, cocking an eyebrow. I've confused him. So, I take advantage of his shock by turning the tables.

"Don't separate us. Please. Let me stay here with Franco. I'll…"

"Let me guess," he says with a coarse bark of laughter. Just like that, he's composed once again, all emotion contained. His hand continues toward me as he hooks his thumb around the neckline of my dress. He tugs on the fabric, coming dangerously close to a stiffening nipple that I can't disguise. "You'll do anything. I think you're addicted to gambling, chica, and you have few bargaining chips left."

He's right, but the stakes are too high to back down now.

"I will," I croak without dwelling on the potential consequences. I reach up, fingering the neckline of my nightgown inches from his position. Is sex what he wants? So be it. "Name your price, Jaguar. Just keep me with him. *Me*, not your men who boast about how Braulio is a dead man in front of him—"

I watch him like a hawk to see how he reacts. His jaw clenches with barely-concealed anger, and he pulls his hand away. Apparently, his men's gossip hadn't been sanctioned by him.

"You can return to your harem as you please," I add in a rush, "but let me stay with him."

"And for that, you'll do *anything*." He runs his thumb along my chin, tilting it for his inspection. "I can work with that. First, get dressed. As for your petty insinuation, no, I did not tell my men to mention anything regarding Braulio around the boy. They'll pay for that."

His voice is rife with rage—his gaze is murderous. I almost feel bad for the unknown goons I've gotten in trouble. Nonetheless, I stiffen at the latest challenge he's presented me with. Get dressed. How? "There is no clothing for me in here," I admit after a hard swallow. To be sure, I peek inside the barren closet one more time. There isn't so much as a pair of shoes inside it.

"Of course, there isn't." He sounds so damn smug at having ripped the rug out from under me. "This isn't your room. I had you put here until you woke up, but you will sleep somewhere else. Come."

His curt nod beckons me forward, and I follow him, numb with fear. At the other end of the stairwell, he opens another door nearly parallel to Franco's room. A sick, twisted part of me notes that it's well beyond earshot of the boy. Could that be why he supposedly chose it for me?

As he opens the door, I brace myself to find a cage, or chains—or perhaps, Gatita growling with hunger and ready to devour me whole.

Instead…

This room has a massive bed draped in black sheets, and floor-to-ceiling windows providing a breathtaking view of the mountainous landscape beyond the property. All in all, it's beautiful, and a world apart from his communal harem rooms.

Stunned, I follow him into another walk-in closet.

"Ladies first," he grates near the threshold. As I slip in front of him, I feel the shape of his hand graze my ass, lingering along my thigh. I can barely silence a groan through clenched teeth. Damn him. Heat unfurls in my belly, only growing hotter as I realize that his bulk traps me like prison bars.

A horrible truth hits me there, surrounded by dark clothing smelling of masculine musk. The plain shirts and slacks hanging from most of the hangers are obviously his.

"This is your room," I croak.

"Look again," he commands.

On my second frantic perusal of the space, I make another chilling discovery—on the other side is a collection of lighter, delicate dresses and shirts. They're more modest than what he dresses his harem in.

Confused, I croak out, "What is this?"

When I pivot to face him, I find Jaguar's expression deceptively blank. Others might mistake his mood for calm, but I know better. He's riled up, hungry for blood. Even his tone feels sharp enough to slice through flesh and bone.

"This is *our* room," he declares. "I thought you'd be happy. You don't have to share with my harem women. Just me. I think I like you in my clothing better, but for now, you should dress in something suitable for Francisco, no?" After reaching for a hanger, he displays the outfit for my approval. "This."

A red dress, flirty in style, with a modest neckline and flowy skirt. Accepting it, I allow him to show me into the attached bathroom.

It's luxurious, of course, composed of gray marble and glistening metal fixtures. Sharing this space with him makes my stomach turn. It is a good thing, then, that I am gaining a greater understanding of Julian Domingas' mind games. He doesn't actually plan to stay here overnight.

He's just testing me.

So why give in to the fear?

Hours after my initial awakening, my mind is fully clear of whatever drug he administered, and I feel less prone to panic. As I approach the walk-in shower, I aim to put on a good show for him. Chin in the air, I gather the skirt of my nightgown, preparing to pull it off over my head.

"Damn." I've barely gone a step when his voice rings out behind me, thick with approval. Before I can even think to turn, I sense him behind me. What feels like a finger grazes the flesh of my lower back, coming dangerously close to a healing wound.

Dios mió, the things this man arouses in me. Electricity prickles beneath my skin, ignited by the harsh, steady sound of his breathing.

"Your back is healing nicely, chica," he remarks, fingering a path toward my ass. Right before contacting that particular part of my body, he withdraws. "Though, I think I will miss those marks when they finally fade. A pity."

Sucking in a breath, I step behind a wall of glass and pretend that it provides more than a temporary barrier between us. As long as I'm hidden here, he can't touch me.

"You could always get your own to admire," I manage to choke out while stripping the nightgown completely. My fingers shake as I toss it aside and turn on the water. It pours from an overhead faucet, deliciously hot. As my muscles relax beneath the spray, I hunt for a washcloth and find one on a shelf built into the wall, just beyond the water's reach, along with a bottle of bodywash.

"Oh?" Jaguar asks, his voice rumbling.

"Yes," I say, biting my lip as my brain taunts me with a mental image of him adorned in claw marks. "Either a tattoo or the real deal. Both would look magnificent on your body, and I'm sure your Gatita is always eager to make new art."

"Ah, but I much prefer to view such designs on you, Lupe. Why should my kitty have all the fun? Next time, I might be the one to paint that beautiful body in red."

I glance over and spy his shadow in the doorway. Damn him.

"Where did you get your kitty, anyway?" I ask him while wrestling with the cap of the bottle. I can't get the damn thing open, and I nearly drop it as I try. "I doubt you found her at the typical animal rescue."

"Oh no, she's imported." A rare note of pride slips into his voice, softening the gruff baritone. It's clear already just how much genuine love he has for the creature. "Straight from the jungle. She was already four when she came here and spicy as hell. Much like you, in fact. It was a battle to tame my girl, I will admit, but well worth it in the end. She is a companion unlike any other."

"And I'm sure you lavish affection on her," I say, hating how my voice trembles in comparison to his.

"Affection, yes. But what is true love without discipline? Respect in any relationship must be earned through proven loyalty—" Above the rushing water, I hear a hiss of fabric, as though he's shed his clothing and tossed it aside. Shirt first. Then the heavier material of his pants.

I hate my brain for how it skips ahead, envisioning the sculpted body left bare. *Damn it.* My heart races with every telltale noise, and I nearly drop the bottle of bodywash again. Gripping it tightly, I force myself to ask, "And how did you do that?"

"What a question." He issues a rasping chuckle I feel resonate down to my core. I'm suddenly aware of how vulnerable I am with my back to him, my naked body on display. I can only imagine his expression—teeth bared, tongue sliding along his lower lip as he takes in the healing wounds he loves so much. "How else does one break a beautiful, strong-willed creature? With patience, of course, and a firm hand. I bought my baby from a dealer who used shipments of animals to smuggle his illicit goods. My Gatita would have been destined for a life mounted on his wall if I didn't bargain for her. One could say that I saved her from a dangerous man who saw her only as a trophy. She *needed* me. Sound familiar?"

His mocking inflection makes the hair on the back of my neck stand on end. *Careful, Pita.* I risk remaining silent for the few precious seconds it takes to wrestle my expression into submission. I can't let him see my fear—and *Dios mío*, am I afraid. Our dynamic has shifted with Franco's arrival.

No longer is this a game with only my life at stake.

"A beautiful story," I say once I regain control of my breathing.

"That's all? You've been so quiet this morning, Lupe. Don't tell me you've grown shy all of a sudden," Jaguar taunts amid the thud of an advancing footstep. "I'm starting to miss your spicy tongue."

"How long do you plan on staying away from your harem?" I ask him, forcing a casual playfulness into my voice. I think I fail at it. "I'm sure they're starting to miss you. I'd hate to bore you. One woman alone certainly can't contain such a healthy sexual appetite."

I'm pleased with myself, convinced I'm saying all the right things.

When I peek over my shoulder, his face is in shadow. His body, however, is on stark display—rippling muscle adorned with indigo tattoos that continue beneath the waistband of his boxers.

He takes his time, hooking his thumb around the elastic. Then our eyes meet as he slowly lets the material fall.

I can't help myself, tearing my gaze away to track the fabric's descent.

My imagination hadn't come close. His cock is already stirring to life from beneath a thatch of dark hair, every bit as imposing as his beloved feline. The flesh seems to tighten more every second I gape, as if he's loving my slack-jawed response. Suddenly, he cups the shaft as I watch, wielding that part of himself like a weapon he's aching to use.

I blame biology alone for how my body reacts to the display—my nipples tighten, and it's ten times harder to breathe. An ache builds between my legs that I try my damn hardest to ignore.

"You seem very eager for me to fly back to my harem," he remarks, and I swear I can feel his gaze tracking the way I press my knees together. "After riding my cock, so desperate to get your son, once you have him in your grasp, it seems you have no use for me after all."

He's right. But wasn't that how this was always supposed to work? I'd debase myself for a taste of his power and influence. He'd toss me a few crumbs, and then bore of me.

Tit for tat. Before this mess began, Pedro said I wouldn't last a week, and thank the heavens we're already past that unofficial deadline.

"You are a man who can't be claimed or tamed by any woman," I point out while setting my bottle aside. With the rag, I work up at lather and rub it along my arms and legs.

"You think you can tame me?" His inflection dips, and I envision him getting a glimpse of my bare ass.

Why the thought makes my belly quiver, I'll never know.

"I would love to see you try, Lupe. Very fucking much."

Dios mío. My eyelids flutter at the grit in his voice. I have to suck in air just to keep focused. "No," I croak. "To be clear, I respect that you can't be controlled. In fact, I encourage your freedom. Don't waste any more time than you need to. I can take care of Franco from here on out."

"Oh, you can, can you?" I'm caught off guard by the bite of amusement in his voice. "And how do you intend to do that?"

With my eyes on the beautiful, modern marble wall in front of me, I try to come up with an answer. "I have money saved up," I lie. That money was won on a whim at the event I met him. Thankfully, it's enough to secure a place somewhere and plot my next steps. In my mind, anyway.

"That's all?" Another advancing footfall snaps me back to the present reality—one where Jaguar is gaining ground, and I have nowhere to run.

"A measly hundred k," he remarks with a sigh. God, he sounds even closer—then I feel him. Just a delicate touch trailing up and down my inner thigh. My startled gasp is easily drowned out as he continues to speak, "That won't be enough to get fake documents for your son. At least more convincing ones than the phonies you've already procured for yourself. Maria Ana Theresa Ramirez. You certainly do love your fake aliases, don't you, *Lupita*."

What feels like the harsh pad of his thumb ghosts between my legs, making me gasp. The hardness of his body presses into me from behind. My skin tingles as his arm comes around me. I have to grind my teeth and stiffen my shoulders to keep from relaxing into his embrace.

"Hmm?" he prods, referring to his unanswered question.

"Y-Yes," I choke out. From this angle, I can't see his expression—and my curiosity kills me. "They've gotten me this far."

"Yes..." That thumb presses into me a fraction harder, sending sparks down my spine. "You won't make it much farther with shoddy documents like that, especially with a child. You'll need to ensure they can pass enough scrutiny for him to enroll in school, of course. You do want him to go to school, don't you?"

"What game are you playing?" I demand. "You don't really care. Just... Just let me rebuild our lives in peace."

"Oh, but that's what I'm getting at," he adds. His hand lands on my shoulder, spinning me to face him. His eyes blaze, as serious as ever. "You won't find *peace* away from me. I've kept this little tidbit of information to myself, but I think it's time you know the full extent of the danger you're in. I'm afraid that the second you decide to leave my orbit, chica, only death awaits you. A rather nasty one, I'm sure. The killer will love to take their time with you."

"W-What?" A cold, finite dread washes over me at such an open threat. Am I surprised? Of course not. Men like Braulio, Jaguar, and Diego… They are all one and the same.

"If you intend to threaten me, Jaguar, I prefer you do so outright and save the mind games for a woman who hasn't heard it all before."

I sound so bitter. So damn hard.

"Exactly." With narrowed eyes, he steps closer. "So, it should come as no surprise to you that someone wants you dead, Lupe. Those butterflies in your apartment were merely the start. They've had you followed, even to my home. They've had spies paid to watch you. All this time, you haven't even noticed, have you?"

But I have. I just assumed he was the source behind the growing sense that I was being watched at every turn.

"The methods are too subtle for Braulio alone," Jaguar adds, reaching out to finger a lock of my hair. Around and around, he manipulates that curl, and I feel like it's a visual metaphor for what he aims to do to me. Corrupt and control. "I'm sure you realize that. He must be working with someone else. *This* man is a pro. He knows who to hire and how to stay under the radar. In fact, it's how I might have gone about it."

Damn this man and his word games. "What are you saying?"

He twists my hair one last time and then tugs, yanking my face closer to his. "I'm saying that they won't stop until they gain control of you. That attack on Braulio's California Villa? I didn't tell you that we captured one of the intruders alive. According to him, they never wanted to kill your son. Their aim was to take him alive—and he was a professional bastard who excelled at his job, too. Ex-military and the whole fucking cocktail. I think they were after Franco only to get to you."

Or the real Tiena. *Dios mío*, what the hell has she gotten herself into?

"So what? I have to stay with you?" I manage to choke out.

"No—" He frowns as if I suggested I jump from the roof. "You should be *begging* to stay with me. I am the only one capable of helping you out of such a dicey predicament, chica. Unless, you were thinking of running to your friend Pedro Juarez for help? I think even he might be limited in this instance—"

"No!" I wrench out of his grasp. "Pedro." I can't hide the terror I know distorts my expression. My hands are in fists, my logic gone. "If you hurt him, I will—"

"Remember who you are talking to," he scolds, but when he captures my chin, his touch is unnervingly gentle. He strokes me, following the curve of my lower lip with a slow, sensual caress. "You play the role of a mindless harlot so damn well, but when pushed to the brink, those claws come out. That's the thing I like about you, my Lupe. When it comes to those you love, truly love, you are fiercely loyal, ready to fight anything and anyone at a moment's notice. If

I had even looked at your son the wrong way, I'm sure you would have lunged for my throat, wouldn't you have?"

He chuckles. He finds the prospect funny.

Tears prickle my eyes as I realize how hopelessly deranged this all is instead. God, I should have never come to him.

"The past lover you mentioned. The one you jumped out of a second-story window to confront. He must have done something monstrous to turn you against him," Jaguar adds. "Perhaps he beat you, or had other women on the side. In any case, he burned you bad, sweetheart. So badly that a part of you, deep down, still loves him."

I try to rip my chin from his grasp. "I don't love any man—"

"Liar," Jaguar scolds, wagging a disapproving finger. He lets me retreat to the back corner of the shower stall, but he remains in the center, effectively trapping me inside it with no way out. "You are capable of it. More than capable. You know, talking to your friend Pedro clarified a few things—"

"If you hurt him…" God. I close my eyes against the bloodied images that pop into my head. Pedro stabbed. Beaten. Torn apart by Gatita. If he's even received a papercut because of me, I'd never forgive myself. "Please tell me you didn't hurt him."

Though even if he hadn't, Pedro most likely came clean and told him the whole truth. He would have had no choice. Oh, God. I feel sick.

"I was intrigued as to whether your protective mother ruse was all an act," Jaguar continues. "But seeing you with your *son*? Ah, that gave it all away. The *truth* about you, chica."

I swear my soul leaves my body. Sheer pride is the only reason I'm still standing, trying to find the words to defend myself—if only for Franco's sake. "I had no choice—"

"Didn't you?" Jaguar asks. I open my eyes to find him stroking his chin. "I had a mother once. I've seen them in action. You women are cut from the same cloth. The creatures you birth are toys to you," his tone turns so cutting I flinch. "Or shields. Only movies portray that relationship any differently. Any bitch can give birth, but when I saw you with your son, I knew."

I swallow, feeling as though I'm choking. God, I wish he would just cut to the chase. Is begging what he craves? Fine, I'll give it to him. "Please don't take me from him—"

"Five fucking minutes of seeing you with him, and I realized that you are an abnormality—" His voice deepens, radiating true anger, and my entire life flashes before my eyes. Franco. Tiena. Diego. All of it.

I barely notice when Jaguar encircles my throat with one hand, teasing the column of flesh with the very tips of his fingers. "All this time, I'll admit that I thought he was just a bargaining chip to you. A way for you to play on my supposed sympathies and wind me up. Once you got the boy, you'd ask me for money. For property. For shoes and cars. You might have gone about your motives in a different way from most, but at the end of the day, you were the same. And believe me, chica. I have seen women sell their children on the side of the road for a dime bag. I have witnessed hundreds of 'mothers' in action. Most would let me lock their sons in Gatita's cage if I asked to—"

I wrench out of his grasp, raising a trembling hand to ward him off. "If you hurt him, I will—"

"Again, with the threats," he growls, snatching my fingers in a punishing grip. "But they aren't always so empty when it comes to you, are they, Lupe? No. You would have backed them up last night if you thought I had any ill will toward Francisco. You would have lunged across the table for my throat, oh don't think I don't realize that—" I can't silence a cry as he pulls me toward him, forcing our bodies to collide.

"You would have. In fact, your friend Pedro told me everything you were willing to do for him. Debase yourself. Come to me on your hands and knees using aliases he supplied you with merely to get to me. I can respect that. What I *can't* respect? Are the lies."

I squeeze my eyes shut. God, poor Pedro. Poor Franco. What have I done?

"Jaguar, please. I had no choice—"

"You had a choice," he says over me, his mouth harsh against my ear. "That's the strange part. You always had a choice to walk away. To cut and run. Other women have made that decision easily with far less to lose than you. Instead, you chose to fight for him."

Wait...

"But in doing so, sweetheart, you wrote a check that magic pussy and spicy tongue can't cash. You promised yourself to me, but you were never really on the table. Isn't that so?"

I look at the damp floor. The wall. The grayish ceiling—anywhere but at him.

"Answer me, Lupe."

My lips part, but nothing comes out, earning a harsh hiss from him. "Look at me, Lupe."

Dios mío. I can't. My hands are shaking, my stomach in knots. As my bare feet twitch against the floor, I consider running.

But, as if anticipating my every move, he's already shifting toward me, caging my body even closer to the wall. "Answer me!"

My head jerks up, and I find his eyes so haunting I'm drowning in them. Never in my life have I been this afraid. Never.

The truly terrifying part? He has yet to lay a single hand on me.

"I… You don't need a woman like me," I croak. "You have your harem. You're happy with them."

"Ah." He strokes the damp hair from my face and flashes a lifeless smile that doesn't reach his eyes. Those dark, endless orbs betray a glimpse of the man he truly is. Not a playful, carefree bachelor, but a calculating predator intent on his prey. "You do have a way with words. For now, I'll let you escape punishment for lying to my face so boldly, chica. But as for our bargain, I still need to be paid. I've decided what you can do to make things right. After all, you've done it once, so it should be no real trouble on your part to do the same for me."

I brace myself for a demeaning command. "Done what?"

"Claimed Braulio's son as your own." He smiles as he says, "So you should have no problem raising one of mine."

CHAPTER THREE

"A son," I croak. Am I surprised the man has children? Hell no. "Where is he? Playing with Franco? I'm sure his mother is waiting for us as well."

I wouldn't be surprised if he sprung an entire happy family on me, out of the blue, complete with the family dog.

"No." He smirks as if amused by a joke I missed. "He would need to be born first, chica. Right from that pretty pussy of yours."

I swallow, too stunned to speak.

"*You* would be his mother," Jaguar continues, driving his point home. "No one else."

Dios mío… Lightheaded, I lean against the wall, praying my wobbling knees hold me upright. I'm hallucinating. Better yet, I'm still delirious from whatever Jaguar drugged me with, and this entire conversation is a fever dream caused by the aftereffects of that. This isn't happening.

It can't be.

"You… You don't want a baby," I rasp, risking a glance in his direction. "Very funny."

Rather than chuckle, pleased I've caught on to his joke, Jaguar doesn't even crack a smile. *Oh no.* I recognize this look. His charming mask has completely fallen off, revealing the calculating figure I first met in his private library. The intellect behind the power-hungry narco.

A man who doesn't ever lie.

"I wouldn't jump to such presumptions, Lupe," he warns. "After all, you were willing to die just to prove how much you value concrete evidence. Give me more respect than that."

Shit.

"I mean…" I shift away from him, clinging to the frigid wall of the stall. "I'm sure you have children already. You have so many women—"

"Those women are not worthy to bear my child," he snaps, advancing a single step as if to drive that statement home. Because someone like him—a man who values his dead brother and keeps a "kitty" he shows more affection to than most humans—would be discerning when it came to any children he would choose to have. "They are whores. The mother of my child would be willing to fight like hell to defend them. She'd protect my seed with her very life. And it doesn't hurt that you have such a pretty little smile—" He reaches out to gently pat my cheek. "Do this for me, and you will have my protection for life—I promise you that."

It isn't lost on me that just days ago, I would have given anything to hear those words.

But now…

"I can't have a child with a man I don't know," I say, aware of his calloused palm against my jawline. One wrong move, and he could easily hurt me. "It wouldn't be right. It wouldn't be fair to you—"

"Fair?" He steps back, letting his hand fall. "You'd sell your body to a stranger for Braulio's son."

"I had no choice," I stammer in a rush. For *Braulio's son*. His grated tone makes it clear that he voiced that distinction on purpose. My façade as Tiena has completely fallen away, and I only have the truth to cling to—and I sense that to misstep now would be to lose what little leverage I have. I have no choice but to continue to walk this tightrope.

"Tell me something," he demands, standing unabashedly naked as the water pelts us from above. "Why go through all this bullshit merely for a child? Why?"

I don't like this change in subject. "Because he's my family—"

"Ah, that's the correct answer. Family." He smiles in that beautiful, unsettling way. "Few understand the true meaning of that word. The fierceness needed to protect and defend it. I want a woman who will mother my children like a wild viper-kitty. I've seen you are capable of that. My little chat with your dear friend confirmed it."

"You don't know me," I croak. Though, given what Pedro might have told him, he probably knows far more than I'd like. Too much. "Please tell me you didn't hurt—"

"You might be right about that," he says over me. "Your friend Pedro is a tough nut to crack. He is just as fiercely protective of you as you are of him. Such loyalty is rarely reciprocal. It means you must be a good judge of character."

"Just tell me if you hurt him. Is he… Please—"

"Pedro is alive and well." Jaguar smiles again, and just like that, his mask is back in place, obscuring his true emotions. "In fact, you can speak to him," he says. "He's downstairs."

My heart sinks further. Downstairs as in a cage, awaiting another iteration of Gatita to rip him apart?

"If you laid even a hand on him—"

"Save your threats." With a wave of his hand, he heads for the exit, pausing only to grab a towel and sling it around his waist. "I'm beginning to understand you now, Lupe. What pushes your buttons, and what keeps you sweet. You don't like being challenged. You don't like feeling as though you have no options. I push you too far, and you will gladly cut and run. But if I give you a reason to stay… Ah, that loyalty—" he snaps his fingers, and the sound haunts me, echoing off the walls. "That will kick in and make you willing to listen. Finish up and get dressed. We'll be waiting for you downstairs. I promised Franco I would take him out on the town today. You will accompany us."

"Wait…"

He's gone before I can fully question him, not that I can find the voice to. In one go, he's rattled so many of the fragile tenants of my life I'd been clinging to. Pedro. Franco. My soul. I feel battered irreparably, left to navigate the aftermath of a wild storm alone.

But I am not alone. I brought two innocent people along with me into this mess. Thinking of them now, I finally wash myself clean.

Focus, Pita. Jaguar thinks he's startled me into submission, but he hasn't. I'm not willing to lie down just yet. There is a way out of this mess. I just need to find it.

My first instinct is to rush downstairs still dripping wet—but I stop myself. With renewed determination, I rinse off and get dressed in the red ensemble Jaguar picked out. My shaking fingers can barely grip the material, but I force myself to keep moving. More important than my, or even Pedro's welfare, is one promise I make to myself then and there—I can't let Franco know we're in danger.

To maintain this fragile balance, I must play my role in Jaguar's twisted game. So, I take the time to dry my hair properly and arrange it into a low bun. Then I pinch some semblance of color into my cheeks.

The woman gaping at me from the mirror is unrecognizable. She seems fragile with her sallow skin and delicate features—but there is a fire in her eyes no one can deny. She isn't broken yet. With a deep breath for courage, I finally leave the bathroom.

The bedroom is empty, devoid of a mocking Jaguar. He isn't in the hallway either, and as I descend the stairs, I spy a figure that makes me stop dead in my tracks. An unfamiliar man, dressed in a gray hoodie and sweats, is waiting for me at the bottom of the staircase. Instantly, all my resolve goes out the window.

Jaguar, that bastard, lied to me, and I fell for his trap like a fool. He's toyed with my patience and taken Franco away while I dallied and sent one of his goons to beat me into submission. I'll never see my poor boy again. I'll...

"Pita?"

I flinch at the use of my name and grip the banister while eyeing the figure below. Rather than approach me menacingly, the stranger has his head angled in my direction, allowing me to see his face. He's surprisingly beautiful for hired narco muscle. "Is that you? Thank God!"

That voice... I squint and recognize a familiar beauty lurking within those masculine features. While they're not caked in a layer of makeup, I'd know those green eyes anywhere.

"Pedro!" I run to him, nearly tripping down the stairs. He's there to catch me, already wrapping me in his arms. I submit to the embrace, blinking back tears—until I remember the sore wounds on my lower back. I pray he doesn't see me wince as I pull back. Desperate to maintain contact with him anyway, I paw at his hoodie, hunting for any wounds he might sport beneath it.

"I was so worried. Did he hurt you? Pedro, I am so sorry. I'm so sorry—"

"I'm okay," he insists, cupping my face in his hands. "Slow down, honey. I'm a bit worse for wear due to having to travel incognito, but fine otherwise. Frankly, I think I look better than you do. You look like shit, Pita."

He's right—but doesn't even know half of it.

"I don't understand." As I examine him, I grow increasingly confused when I don't find even a scratch. "He said he questioned you."

I know firsthand the danger that can entail.

"He did," Pedro says carefully. When I reach for his arm again, he gently seizes my wrist. "I thought I was meeting with a client of mine, only when I got to the venue, Julian fucking Domingas was there instead. To say I almost shit myself would be an understatement."

His eyes show fear his voice doesn't. God, I can only imagine what he's been through.

"I thought I was dead, to be honest, Pita. I've heard the rumors, you know?"

Rumors I'd had confirmed with painful certainty.

With more fervor than before, I tear at his clothing and start to lift his shirt. "Did he hurt you? God, I'll never forgive myself—"

"No. No…" He shrugs me off. "He did confirm something for me, though. Pita, do you have any idea what the hell is going on? Tiena is a selfish bitch, but she doesn't cut and run unless shit gets too hot. Like with—" He breaks off with a grimace, but my mind finishes that statement for him.

Like with Diego. She saw the danger coming before I ever did. Rather than warn me, she left the damn country. She left me.

To be fair, I'm sure Pedro saw the horror coming as well. The difference? He stayed by my side to face it with me, and for that, I will never forsake him.

"Tiena is the least of my problems right now," I admit, grabbing his hand. "All I care about is you and Franco—"

"The point is, I should have seen it before, but the signs are there, honey," Pedro says with a tremor in his voice. "It might be crazy, but I think… Honey, I think Diego could be back."

"Great. Fucking great." I choke out a watery laugh and find myself wandering into a nearby room, desperate for fresh air. By chance, I've stumbled toward the doors to the terrace and step outside with Pedro on my heels.

"Christ," he remarks, impressed. "This place must be at least several mil. Life-threatening danger aside, you think you can get me in touch with his agent? I've been working on my latest conquest, and if he bought me a house like this, I'd do all the freaky shit he wants me to. There's this thing with a hair dryer and jump rope that he's been begging to—"

"It isn't mine," I say, cringing at the insinuation. "This isn't a vacation, Pedro. God, it's gone way too far. I should just leave. We can grab Franco and run."

"Relax, Pita. I didn't mean it like that." Pedro sighs. "As for Jaguar, I just told him the truth. About us. Your past. While I took some 'creative liberties,' he didn't seem to question it. I was wondering if you'd told him any of it yourself."

I whirl on him. "You told him that I shot my ex-boyfriend in the head with a stolen pistol and then took the five hundred dollars we found in his apartment to pay a coyote to get me to Texas before his boys could track me down and gut me?" For a second, I forget myself, and my voice raises in pitch. "Did you tell him about how we had to fake my death by using the body of some poor drug mule he'd already killed that night? Or did you talk about how my own fucking sister made me grovel for her protection and used me to smuggle drugs in a backpack for her twisted narco lover before I had the balls to put my foot down?"

Anger makes my voice shake. I'm shouting. If Jaguar is nearby, he'll be able to hear every word.

"No," Pedro says, wincing. He reaches for me, his movements gentle. "I didn't jump to the good part. You're shaking, honey. Come here." He draws me into another hug, and I relent to it, relishing his comforting warmth.

"You don't smell nice," I point out, my nostrils wrinkling. "What is with this look, anyway—" I tug on the sleeve of his hoodie. "You used to say you'd drop dead rather than wear polyester."

He laughs. "Don't be silly, *puta*. This is me being incognito. I couldn't risk anyone tracking me out here. Your friend Jaguar made that very clear. The bastard even took my phone, though he promised to return it the second I return to Texas. Thank God. I know Chico, one of my regulars, is probably blowing up my inbox right now."

I look at his face and see more fear threatening to break through his fracturing mask of calm.

"So, what did you really tell him?" I ask.

"I told him about the only subject he seemed interested in —you. I said that when you love, you love hard. And when you hate someone, they deserve it."

"Like Diego?" I manage a weak smile, but Pedro grimaces.

"Hell yes, but I didn't mention that *puta*." He scoffs. "I made it clear that you had no ill will toward Jaguar. That you only wanted his protection for Franco."

"It sounds like a fairy tale to me. You think he believed it?"

Pedro winks. "My skills for persuasion are unmatched, honey. Of course, he bought it. Hook. Line. Sinker."

"If that's the case, why do you look so terrified, Pedro? Nothing ever scares you. Ever. What's wrong?"

He sighs sadly and fingers a piece of hair that's fallen out of my bun. "I'm worried for you, honey. Even before Jaguar approached me, I've heard things on the grapevine. Rumors about a woman they claim is Tiena—that's why I ignored them at first. But the more I listen, the more obvious it becomes that they aren't talking about a bleached-blond bimbo. They're talking about you. They've exploded ever since you were seen at the cage fight."

"Braulio?" I ask. Deep down, I hope he's the only enemy I have to contend with, but even before Pedro frowns, I already know the answer.

"Thought so at first. Until I heard rumors of a new narco in town. A trafficker able to supply a grade of cocaine so pure a kilo can fetch half a million clean. Shit like that hasn't come from around here. This dealer doesn't have a name he goes by, but those who have interacted with him have chosen a particular moniker. *Eye patch.*"

I feel the color drain from my face. "Oh, God."

"You've heard of him too," Pedro surmises.

But I thought it was a cruel trick. A mind game, perhaps, played at Tiena's expense. Not mine.

"He's back… Oh, God, Pedro—"

"So, what if he is?" My friend places his hands on my shoulders, forcing me to face him. "You have the protection of the most powerful man in the country."

A man I can't risk staying with a second longer. A man who is far more dangerous than he lets on. A man who wants me to bear his child for an insane, demented reason. All of that brings me to only one conclusion.

"I can't stay here, Pedro."

"Did he hurt you, Pita?" His face changes, his eyes narrowing. "What's wrong?"

"I…" *No.* Clenching my teeth, I choke back any confession. The last thing I should do is rope Pedro into another mess. "Don't worry about it. Thank you for coming here… How did you even get here?"

Hours from Texas and the rich, mysterious clients who are his bread and butter.

"Courtesy of Jaguar." Pedro raises an eyebrow. "When the man politely asks that you get on a private jet at his expense, let's just say, one can't exactly refuse. And here I am, pleased to see you've been living it up, at least. Look at you, dressed like a little hot tamale."

I see right through his fake smile. "There is something you aren't telling me. What?"

He sighs, and some of his bravado peels away. Dark circles are under his eyes as if he hasn't slept in days, and his smile is too strained around the edges. I know my friend—he's worried. "Jaguar didn't bring me here on some carefree vacation, Pita. He wants something."

I frown, confused. "Money? Information?"

"No. He wants me to convince you to stay with him."

I brace myself for the other shoe to drop. *Stay with him or else.*

Pedro, however, doesn't seem too eager to deliver a threat. His wide eyes remain fixed on me, and he seems to soften his tone, "He suggested I help you see reason."

"Did he threaten you? Or bribe you?"

"No!" He winces at the insinuation. "He just showed me some very convincing evidence that your life is in danger. There is a bounty on your head, Pita. Not just in Texas. Everywhere. The kind of bounty few men can ignore. The kind of bounty that will draw out every crazy motherfucker from a thousand-mile radius. I'm sorry, honey. But even I can't help you."

"Because of him," I rasp.

"Diego?"

"No. Jaguar. He did this." Anger seethes through my veins, but with every passing second, it feels more plausible. That bastard. "He wants to pressure me to—" I have enough sense to break off without revealing Jaguar's latest impulsive demand.

"Pita? Where are you going?"

I don't know. Anger alone drives me deeper into the house. When a familiar, unsettling voice finally trickles into my ears, I'm in the basement, nearing that game room.

"Another win," Jaguar says, his voice thick with praise. He's so intent on Franco that he doesn't seem to notice—or care —as I march toward his chair, my hand extended. "We'll make a warrior out of you yet—"

"How dare you?" I swear it's like someone else takes over my body. All I can do is watch my fingers fly out and connect with his jaw. *Thwack!*

"Auntie?" Franco whirls to face me with a confused expression, a game controller in hand. "What's wrong?"

"Nothing," Jaguar says. To my utter terror, I realize he's smiling, even as he runs his fingers over his left cheek. As our eyes meet, his tongue shoots out, trailing his lower lip. I can barely smother a gasp as I look away, rushing to smooth my hands over Franco's face.

"I'm okay, baby," I insist, fighting to keep my voice steady. My fake smile fractures as I sense Jaguar shift in his chair. "But I need to speak with Mr. Domingas. Alone."

His skills for deception on clear display, Jaguar doesn't visibly react to the demand. He turns off the game system before suggesting, "Franco, why don't you practice your basketball dribbling? I left the ball outside." With his eyes on me, he sits back, cocking his head in amusement. "This shouldn't take long."

"Okay…" Franco leaves warily, his tiny steps echoing down the hall.

The second they fade from earshot, Jaguar sits forward, threading his fingers together.

"Oh, how you will regret that, Lupe. I don't give a damn what you think of me, but you won't color how that little boy sees me. Understood?"

I bat aside the demand, too confused to wonder why someone as twisted as he is, would care about a child's opinion. That no longer matters. Once I've said what I have to, we're leaving.

"You put a bounty on my head? Have you no damn shame? Do you even care about Franco's safety? How could you?"

His eyes cut to slits, and he lurches to his feet. "Watch yourself, Lupita. It seems your friend Pedro didn't properly relay the information I conveyed to him. I didn't put a bounty on you, but someone did. Someone with a lot of money to burn, chica. They want you alive, though they don't much care as to the condition."

My heart sinks. Blood runs cold. It can't be.

"You're lying."

"I love that spicy little tongue, but call me a liar again, and I will cut it out of that pretty mouth. You don't believe me?" He reaches into his pocket and withdraws a cell phone. After swiping at the screen, he holds it up for me to see.

"Take a look for yourself. It's an encrypted website that some men use to trade bounties on their enemies. I never use it myself. I prefer to take care of my shit directly, but look who a friend of mine happened to find?"

He points to a grainy photo of a woman surrounded by a block of text. Tiena Sanchez, age twenty-three—only the woman in the image has dark hair instead of blond. The height and weight are specific to me as well. Those details aren't what make me sink to my knees and choke on a wave of bile.

Under the heading "aliases," whoever initiated the bounty put just one. Butterfly.

"Oh, God…"

"There is no name listed under who to contact when the deed is done," Jaguar remarks. "Just a number that leads to an automated line. I'm having my men track down the source, but no average *pendejo* is behind this. I don't think Braulio has the money or the balls."

"Franco isn't safe with me," I croak. Hell, at this rate, he might even be safer with Braulio, as cruel as that is to admit. At least he would only have to fear bruises and neglect. Not brutality. Death. "I can't stay near him. They already tried to hurt him once…" I shiver with the weight of the decision. "I need to get him somewhere safe and leave him. I can't—"

"What you need to do is—" Jaguar hooks a hand beneath my arm, wrenching me to my feet. When he spins me to face him, I sway. He has to hold me upright, his strength unwavering. "Not second-guess me. I said that you had my protection, Lupe. You doubt that, and you doubt me. You've already pushed your luck more than once—" He thumbs my bottom lip. "Let's not try my patience any more than you already have."

"Your protection," I say thickly, hating how the word tastes on my tongue. "But to earn it, I have to give my body to you, don't I? Let you impregnate me without my consent. I have to—"

"No. You misunderstood me." He swipes his thumb along my chin, gathering the tears I didn't even realize were falling there. He stares at them as if marveling at the sight. Almost as if he's never taken the time to savor the sobs of his victims before.

"I never said my protection was contingent on sex, or my child. When I plant my seed in you, Lupita, you won't be unwilling. Trust me on that. Count yourself lucky. You've already placed a down payment on my protection. I need a few more things from you to seal the deal. One, you wipe away these tears and show Francisco a good day out. We'll take him to the park. Out for ice cream. Nice, wholesome family shit. My second condition is that you wait until we return to Texas to dredge up these nasty little rumors. We won't reveal that darkness in front of him. *Claro?* And then…" He leans in, his voice low. "Then, I will punish you for this and take my time doing so."

His tone chills me to the core, his expression equally terrifying. Yet I don't feel an ounce of fear as I tilt my head back to hold his stare. Why is that?

Maybe my newfound bravery has something to do with how his smile has widened. Cut to slits, his eyes rove over me, zoning in on my body like a man shamelessly taking stock of property he owns.

I feel myself flush, as the air thickens in my lungs. I can't stop my teeth from seizing my lower lip to shut myself up.

Jaguar chuckles. He's loving this, savoring getting a rise out of me. As if to reward me, he reaches around me to cup my ass, groping harshly through the thin fabric. Gasping, I'm thrown against him, forced to cling to his forearms for balance. The thick muscle twitches beneath me like a hungry predator, desperate to consume me whole.

"Do you hear me?" he asks against my ear. "I want you to confirm that you do."

"I understand," I tell him, righting myself as his hand falls away. "But I have a condition of my own. When we have our 'conversation,' you tell me everything. Exactly what you're planning. Having you toy with my life is one thing, but not Franco's. He could be at risk because of me. I need to know you understand that. *Claro?*"

"Crystal, chica," he says, patting my cheek. Then he snatches a fistful of his black shirt and dabs at my sore, still-leaking eyes. "We'll hold off on each other for now. A truce of sorts. But damn… Am I going to enjoy taking my retribution out of your pretty little skin. There—" He steps back and lets his shirt fall. "All better. Let's go."

He extends his hand for mine, and I'm startled by how quickly I reach for it—despite the threats and the fear crawling beneath my skin. Despite the look in his eye that very much promises retribution.

A part of me can't deny that even at his worst, the man has a quality about him that demands trust.

Even though I know I will regret giving him an ounce of it.

CHAPTER FOUR

When we finally leave the house, I'm struck by how different this moment is from the previous times I've gone out with Jaguar. We're devoid of his usual entourage, for one, accompanied only by Horatio and a stern-faced driver who commands the sleek SUV we find waiting in a circular driveway out front.

It isn't lost on me just how different he is without his posse to perform for. He drops some of his swagger, but rather than diminish him, he stands taller, radiating confidence I can't deny. Damn him. He's mesmerizing.

"Pedro will not be joining us," Jaguar says, explaining his absence. "I've arranged for him to be entertained while we're gone. Don't worry, Lupe—" He reaches out to run his knuckles against my cheek. "A friend of yours is a friend of mine."

That doesn't sound like a good thing. My stomach churns ominously, but I stop myself from looking back and hunting for any sign of Pedro on the property. It's what he wants me to do. Visually show fear. Doubt him. Give him a reason to push my buttons and test my patience.

So, I smile and reach for the tiny figure walking on the other side of him.

"What would you like to do today, Franco?" I ask, pulling him close to me. As close as I possibly can. I tighten my grip on his hand so he can't wiggle away and ensure I sit beside him in the back seat. Not Jaguar.

"Go on," Jaguar prods, his tone dangerously soft—a warning. "This is your day. Tell us what you'd like to do. Whatever it is, I'll make it happen."

"Really?" Franco looks from Jaguar to me, his brown eyes comically wide. "Can we do mini golf? I always wanted to go."

I wince at the pleading note in his voice.

"Of course!" Jaguar laughs. "Mini golf it is. Let's see if you can beat me by the end."

The car takes off while I sweat in terror. If there is a bounty on me, traipsing out in the open seems like the worst possible thing to do. I feel like there's a target on my forehead, and everyone around me is in mortal danger.

Even Jaguar.

Though, for all the attention he pays to me, I might as well be invisible. Franco has his full focus. They joke together.

Laugh. Chat about video games utilizing terms I don't even understand.

When we reach a colorful play center bursting with activities, they take off, leaving me to catch up with Horatio. As surly as ever, the guard plods along beside me without any acknowledgment. At least until he inclines his head my way without warning.

"You don't need to be afraid," he says. His voice is so gruff I can barely make out the individual words, but I sense that he rarely makes an effort to speak to anyone apart from Jaguar.

"Of?" I ask.

In response, the man cuts his eyes to the two figures bounding ahead of us, trading jokes and laughter so freely that I'm gritting my teeth watching them. Is this jealousy I'm feeling? Or relief…?

"He's good with the boy," Horatio mutters. "You don't need to be worried."

I open my mouth to respond but wind up saying nothing. Instead, I copy Horatio and just watch the man in question interacting with a child less than half his size. As Franco chatters excitedly, Jaguar reaches down and ruffles his hair. I rock onto the tips of my toes, but I suppress the urge to intervene. Heart in my throat, I merely watch. Jaguar himself draws the most attention, from not just me. I can't deny that the man cuts a bold figure, decked out in black, his tattoos in full view, his feral smile… Tamed for once.

That's the scary part. It's not that he's ingratiated himself with Franco nearly to needle me.

It's that he seems to genuinely enjoy doing so. Much like he'd been in the game room, he's stern with him at times, but always gentle. He fosters a friendly rivalry when they play but never lets Franco get out of hand or too upset. He never lets him win, either. He makes him work for his fleeting victories.

He acts like… Well, like his father. A better one than Braulio ever was. Admitting that guts me. I feel like such a bad Aunt, having stood by in silence all these years, convincing myself that it wasn't that bad. After all, Franco had a roof over his head. He had his own bedroom and went to sleep at night with a full belly. He never had to endure the horrors that my sister and I had.

He never had to wake up one day to the grim realization that his parents had sold him to pay off debts. No… Not now. I don't like to think about that—though I was the lucky one. Tiena wasn't always the way she's become. Once, we were truly sisters, who did everything together. Until that terrible day when my sister's joyful innocence was stolen forever.

"You look so sullen, Lupe," Jaguar scolds once we break for lunch. We're seated at a colorful table while Franco stands at an all-you-can-eat ice cream buffet nearby, helping himself to multiple scoops under Horatio's watchful eye. "Remember our bargain? Smile."

"You're too good at this," I tell him hoarsely. "You have your own children. Tell me how many."

Ha ha. The joke's been on me all along.

Taking a deep breath, he answers, "No children." His low tone makes me do a double take—he isn't smug and boastful when it comes to this topic. He's guarded as hell. Sensing my curiosity, he winks. "At least, none *yet*. Don't be naughty now. Put on that smile. Franco deserves one fun day, don't you think?"

Because he's preparing him to face a storm of bad ones. That's why he's trying so hard and doting on him so much. To soften the blow when I'm killed.

Or sold.

Still, Jaguar has a point. I smile wide, and he cradles my chin against his palm in approval.

"That's a good girl," he tells me, his voice sinfully deep as he caresses my jawline with the pad of his thumb. "I almost believe you mean it. Now go put on a convincing show for me."

Wrenching out of his grip, I stand and skip over to the buffet to help Franco make his decision. Once we've eaten, we take a detour to the park, and Franco tires himself out on a jungle gym while Jaguar and I watch from the sidelines like the unworthy pseudo parents that we are.

I haven't let the guilt get to me until now—but when it finally hits, it hits me hard. I don't belong here. Tiena does. This is her child I've stolen away. Her son I've formed my future around. Her life to cherish, wherein Jaguar wouldn't even have a role to play. He'd be relegated to the dark, dangerous men Franco would normally be taught to run from.

What am I doing?

When we return to the house as night falls, I've made up my mind on at least one course of action. Damn Jaguar and his senseless ultimatums. I'll decide what is best for my nephew, and it isn't him.

"Jaguar!" Franco chirps from beside me, rubbing his eyes. "Can we play video games before I go to bed?"

"Oh, I can do better than that," Jaguar promises while helping us out of the SUV.

We head straight to the game room, where Franco gleefully picks up a controller.

"You can play a different game tonight," Jaguar tells him before loading the software. "This one you can play by yourself. Let me know if you beat my score. I need to speak with your mama for a moment."

Uh-oh. Despite the ominous warning laced within those words, I don't hesitate to follow him down the hall and into an adjacent room. It's barren, filled with large cardboard boxes, and dimly lit by only an overhead light. I observe them and miss the moment Jaguar snatches my wrist.

"I warned you." With a bruising grip, he drags me inside, closing the door behind us. "I've let you get away with running that spicy fucking tongue more than once, but I—"

"I'm a liability to him." My voice breaks. I don't even care about facing Jaguar's wrath anymore. "I should have never taken him from Braulio."

"This isn't like you," Jaguar accuses, his breath hot on my throat. "The spicy viper-kitty's lost her edge. This isn't entirely because of that bounty, either, is it?"

"No. It's because I'm the kind of woman who does horrible things," I admit, staring down at my pale fingers. They might as well be covered in blood. "Who attracts the type of men who cause harm and wreak havoc. I can't be trusted to care for a six-year-old child, let alone a baby."

His boast is what truly has unnerved me, if I feel brave enough to admit it. I can't fathom the kind of woman Julian Domingas would deem worthy of having his child. Someone broken, I'm sure. A corrupted vessel.

"What kind of woman causes only pain to those around her?"

Not only to Franco, but Pedro. Perhaps even Tiena. After all, I'm the one who brought Diego into our lives in the first place.

"Franco might have been better off if I let you feed me to your kitty," I tell Jaguar. "So beat me if you have to. You couldn't make me feel any worse than I already do."

"Beat you?" He grabs my chin, forcing me to look into his eyes. "Oh, but I never said that my punishment would result in *pain*, did I, chica? And I never claimed that you wouldn't enjoy it."

He shoves me against the wall, taking care not to put pressure on my injured side. I marvel at the small kindness, but I'm not fooled. In the shadows, his eyes glow with a playful, devious emotion I can't name.

"What was it you asked me before your trip here? Fuck you like my dream woman, and we could be 'even.' Do you really want to know who my dream woman should be?" He chuckles and leans in, bringing his mouth to my ear.

At the same time, he snatches fistfuls of my dress in both hands, wrenching the hem up to my waist.

"My woman is bold. She doesn't waste her tears on silly matters that don't concern her. Her world ends and begins in our home, and she is the only creature in the world I would trust to bear my children."

He taunts me by dragging a finger between my legs, highlighting my lack of underwear. I gasp, hating the heat that pools automatically in response. It's like his touch alone activates a switch that flips my body on in ways it's never responded to anyone else.

"She would know what that means to me," he grates against my earlobe. "To be the co-creator of my family. The guardian of my seed. She would hold her head high, knowing that she would gladly die for our children. That is what matters to me, Lupe. More than sex. More than pretty little lies. I require action. Loyalty. Honor. You give me those things…"

He enters me with a finger. Then another. I have only seconds to adjust to the intrusion before he withdraws both digits.

"You made it sound as though I expected you to lie down with me in the dirt and birth my child in Gatita's cage. Oh no, I'd give you the world, Lupe."

He grips my throat and nudges my hips into the proper position for him to step in between my spreading thighs.

"You'd have my world inside of you, Lupe. All of me. You'd own me in a way that your ex-lover could never claim. I don't hurt those who belong to me. I worship them. Cherish. I will die for them. And you looked as though I'd sentenced you to death—" He strokes the wayward hair from my face. "No. I gave you a way out of the hell you're living in. I am the only man you will ever need."

My mind is blown by his words. My eyelids feel heavy. My heart is a swollen, frantically beating thing, and I can't suck enough air into my lungs.

What he's describing shouldn't be desirable in the slightest. It's a prison—not a beautiful fantasy. I should know better.

"It wouldn't be all sunshine and roses," he adds, pressing into me further while reaching between us with one hand. "It would be harrowing, at times. I am a busy man…"

The buzz of his zipper edges his words.

"And my woman, she would have her own empire to run. She'd answer to no one in the domain of our home, not even me. She'd oversee our children. My sanctuary. My goddamn soul. All right there in one house. I told myself that no woman could be worthy of such an honor. No one."

His pants fall next—I hear their descent, a soft whisper of fabric on flesh. With my eyes locked on his, I can't look down to see the parts of him left bare.

"Most women in my orbit are selfish creatures, chica. They scurry around, desperate for their bags and their shoes, and their pretty dresses. They would see my child as a paycheck and nothing more. My home would be a trophy. Worthless, all of them. Even those in my harem aren't a prize to me. They are used." He laughs at that admission, though I'd already called him out on that. He parades them like toys on a shelf, merely for display. "But you are too proud to count yourself among them. Too proud to dance at my beck and call for material things. Too damn proud. You don't even see the respect I've extended to you. I don't offer it very often."

I feel him inside me before I'm ready. It's a tight fit, heightened by dangerous friction. I can't silence a gasp, but his hand clamps over my mouth, muffling the noise.

"What I wouldn't give to have you scream for me," he whispers. "So loud you'd make the rafters shake. You have no fucking clue how badly I want that. Crave it. I want to learn just how many different noises little Lupe can make with that magic tongue. But this is good practice, because when our children are old enough—"

He rocks into me, and my eyelids flutter. His mentioning of children makes me painfully aware of Franco in the next room, shouting innocently at his video game.

"Ahh! No, I lost again—"

"We'll have to fuck like this while they are distracted," Jaguar murmurs, commanding my attention. "No noises, sweetheart. No slamming your body against the wall as you take every inch of me inside you. That will be one of the few times we ever go this slow. Quiet. I'll indulge your little fantasy to feel me, and you'll come like a goddamn waterfall."

I shiver at his explicit narration. I should be horrified. Not…

"God, you're so wet," he rasps, sounding angry at the fact. "Even a taste of me isn't punishment to you. You take me so damn well, always so greedy for it. Greedy for me. How deep can you take me from this angle, chica? Like this."

He bucks his hips but never hard enough to make a sound.

My eyes roll. It's sinful pressure, but nowhere near the force I'm used to. An ache begins in my core, spreading throughout my body until I'm shaking with need. God, I need him harder. Faster.

"Be patient," he scolds as if reading my mind. "I need you throbbing for me, Lupe. I've imagined how you'd feel like this, with that magic tongue silenced. God damn, you feel like heaven."

His grated cadence rips through me, and I whine. Forsaking his slow, steady motions, I arch into him, fucking myself on him, using his body to find the leverage I need.

A rumbling growl revs in his chest. "*Fuck*," he snarls. Then he hooks an arm around my waist and snatches me into him.

I swallow the moan that bubbles up my throat. I choke down any other resulting cries of pleasure. This man is so damn cruel. So devious.

He makes me work for this pleasure, until I'm riding him, much like I did when he made me show him what it was like to fuck a man who loved me. This is different. There is no imaginary man to soften the blow.

Julian Domingas is the one inside me, rigid and hard as steel. His breath is what I feel on my throat, and his taste is on my tongue as he replaces his fingers with his lips. We kiss violently. Punishingly. It's a silent rendition of the conversation we need to have.

Something loud and abrasive with shouting and filthy words. Sinful curses. Hateful things I might regret and dirty, wicked promises.

With every stabbing thrust of his tongue, he tells me all the lewd ways he wants to use my body. Where he wants to stick what. How easily he can debase me. How much he can make me enjoy what he does to me. How I'll always beg him for more, even if I'm too proud to admit it.

And with what energy I can muster to match his intensity, I tell him a few things in return. How much I fear him. How much I truly hope his fantasy woman isn't me. How some sick part of me doesn't care about the logistics and wants to be that for him anyway.

His perfect little chica who'd happily tend to his brood. The woman he'd give his life to protect.

God, the man accused me of lying, but he's a better one than I am.

He almost makes me want to believe him.

CHAPTER FIVE

When our senses return, and our breathing slows to normal, we do a dangerous thing. We linger. I can't name exactly how it happens.

Maybe when he doesn't rush to pull himself out of me, and I don't eagerly try to evade his grasp? Pressed against the wall, my face in his hands, we share several, tentative breaths and eye each other. Perhaps the way two stray jaguars in the jungle might while trying to decide if the other is friend or foe.

Or dinner.

In the background, Franco happily and loudly plays his new video game. It seems Jaguar isn't just skilled at manipulating fearful adults, but children with short attention spans. In any case, he knows exactly how to get what he wants.

And for the moment, he seems to want me.

His eyes darken as he recovers first, leaning in to whisper something barely audible into my ear. "We can take your pregnancy off the table for the time being," he tells me while ghosting a hand along my belly to smooth my dress into place. "In the meantime, we must deal with the threat against you. As you like to point out, I am a very patient man. I can wait."

"Mr. Jaguar?" Franco suddenly calls out, seemingly bored with playing alone. "Are you going to watch me? I'm going to beat the score!"

"Of course, you are," Jaguar calls back with a smile. "Just give me a minute to get your mama settled. She's been nagging me to show her the kitchen. See if you can beat my score by the time I get back."

He takes my wrist and pulls me after him to the door. I stagger, still disoriented. God, I can feel him inside me, still dripping along my inner thigh.

I pray Franco doesn't peek from the room as we pass it, and Jaguar hastens me up the stairs.

The kitchen is every bit as luxurious as the rest of the house. Jaguar releases me near a glistening center island while he washes his hands in a large double sink. With his back to me, I can't gauge his reaction.

Do I even want to?

"There is something you haven't been honest about with me, Lupe," he says, speaking normally without fear of

Franco overhearing. "I don't know what it is yet, but you are not naturally inclined to lie. I'm beginning to see that. It makes you jumpy. Reckless. You are confident in your truth, but do you want to know the truly strange part? I can tell that what you're hiding isn't a threat to me. It's not that you're secretly working with Braulio against me or that you aim to steal my money and flee. It's personal to you. A secret that isn't particularly dangerous, but exposing it would make you vulnerable to me in a way you've calculated isn't worth the risk. You think I'll use it against you."

Do I think that? No, not entirely. My past can be used against him, though. Diego is out there waiting for me, and I'm not in a hurry to face him just yet. Not unless I'm provoked to.

"You think I'll tie you down and torture the truth from you," Jaguar adds, his voice dangerously soft. He shakes out his hands and dries them on a nearby towel. "Maybe I would, were you any other woman. Someone who would easily back down at the sight of a whip or chains. But you? I think you'd relish in enduring my brutality, chica. You'd use it as an excuse to hide even more of yourself from me, and I won't make it so easy for you. Oh no. I'll play your game. Give you time to squirm and second-guess everything you say to me. We'll make a thrilling time of it. Just when you think you're ahead, I'll come from behind and claim the victory I'm owed. You can bet your ass on that."

I say nothing, too busy struggling to breathe.

"Oh, what fun we will have. However—" His tone shifts, casual once more. "I've promised Franco I'd play with him first. If you think you can trust me with him for five minutes, you can run up to our room and catch up with Pedro. I left your cell phone there. And if you're worried about leaving me alone with your son, don't be. I arranged for your worries to be placated, Lupe. You see… I understand the importance of having a clear view of a situation from every possible angle. Of knowing every perspective and potential bias. I've learned a lot from reading those books of mine you admire so much. Which reminds me, tomorrow I will show you my new library you can utilize. Now run along."

He heads for the basement, and it takes everything I have not to follow him. I know a challenge when I hear it, and whatever he has in mind must be twisted enough that he craves to enjoy my reaction from afar. So be it.

I'll trust Franco to call if he needs me for the five minutes it takes to race upstairs and into the master bedroom.

Once there, I skid to a stop, too startled to compose myself.

All along, there's been a flat screen hidden in the wall across from the bed. It's in plain view now, displaying a scene that makes me gasp.

It's a series of eight squares, each one containing a different view of the house. The entrance. The outdoor patio. The game room. The room beside it…

And one square image, in particular, makes the hair on the back of my neck stand on end. It's positioned directly at the back door, where I spoke with Pedro about Diego. Dear God. Could he have heard every word we said?

I don't have long to process the chilling prospect. A buzzing sound pierces the air, drawing my attention to the bed where my phone sits, vibrating over the silken sheets. I answer it, unsurprised to find Pedro on the other end.

"Thank God," he says. "I've been worried about you all damn day, but he told me not to call you until—"

"He's probably recording us," I say hoarsely. "So, keep that in mind."

"Shit," Pedro says with genuine alarm. "This is like when I messed with a high-profile politician who was so paranoid about blackmail, he kept his used condoms in a lock box that he would carry around with him. Sick shit, Pita. But even if Jaguar is listening… How are you? You didn't seem like yourself before. I've been worried sick about you, *puta*."

"Didn't I?" The same frantic, paranoid Pita always getting herself into sticky situations.

"Fuck no. You seemed edgy. Restless. You only get like that when shit has hit the fan, and it's out of your control."

"I am always out of control."

"Like hell you are," he says coldly. "You always have a backup plan, and people write you off as a pushover until they realize the truth—you are crazy as hell, and no one gets under your skin easily. This is more than having an old friend coming to visit you out of the blue," he adds, cleverly disguising his reference to Diego.

"I am a shadow, Pedro," I say softly. "Or at least, I am used to living in one. I am always in the background, and I prefer it that way. Every time I think I can step up and take center stage of my own life, everything goes to hell—" My eyes water. "People get hurt. People die."

"Yes," he says. "But sometimes those people are the very ones who sought to hurt you in the first place. Don't forget that. Damn girl. Whatever happened had to be bad. You're rarely this pessimistic."

"I'm worried about Franco," I say, my voice breaking. "You, too."

"Don't be. You'll do what it takes to protect us. I know you, and it will take more than Jaguar to get beneath your defenses. Buck up, Pita. It won't get easier from here."

He's right. And as a sudden noise makes me turn to the doorway, I realize just how prescient he truly is.

"Say goodnight to Pedro," Jaguar says. He leans against the wall, his arms crossed, an eyebrow raised. "You will see him tomorrow. I arranged a spa day, just for the two of you. For now, however, I will commandeer your time."

"I guess I'm dismissed," Pedro says, having overheard. "Don't worry about me, Pita. He set me up in a fucking lush penthouse suite. I'll be good until tomorrow."

"Bye, Pedro," I croak.

But I don't hang up first, and I'm left listening to the silence as Jaguar advances.

"So moody you are, tonight," he says, casting me an appraising glance. "I need to find a way to cheer you up, it seems. Would a new purse or some cash do the trick? Or are you after something more than that?" He laughs loudly, chilling me to the core. "Something tells me you're harder to please than my usual acquaintances, or even dear Francisco."

"It's late." I stand, unwilling to enter another mental sparring match with him. I know that I can only put off the inevitable for so long. I'm desperate enough to take that risk. "I should tuck in Franco for bed—"

"Wait. I want to make sure you understand just how seriously I take your safety, Lupe."

"Oh?"

"Yes." He cups my chin against his palm as he comes closer. "Braulio has turned his people against you, it seems. Should you return to Texas on your own, your life will be at risk. I hope Pedro told you that."

"It's a good thing that you have promised me your protection then," I say hoarsely, wrenching out of his grip. "Goodnight, Jaguar."

To my utter shock, he doesn't try to stop me as I head for the door. He steps aside, but his voice chases me into the hall.

"When you return, we will discuss where he will be safest. Since you don't trust him to me. There are schools I've looked into. You can have the final say."

My steps falter, and I feel along the wall for balance. I don't know how to process that. It could be a threat to separate me from Franco or a sign that he's listened to my concerns. In any case, he's right. Franco isn't safe with me, not until I look into whether Diego or someone else wants me dead.

For now, I push those fears from my mind as I find Franco in his bedroom and help him get ready. He's so tired he submits to a long hug and lets me tuck him beneath his blankets.

"Honey," I ask, as he settles in. "How would you feel about going to school a few weeks early? A nice one with plenty of other boys to play with, and I could visit you there whenever you wanted. How is that?"

Around a yawn, he asks, "What about my papa? And mama? Will they come too?"

"I don't know, sweetheart," I say. "You know I won't lie to you, and things are… Complicated right now. I'm so sorry."

He says nothing, choosing to close his eyes instead.

After shutting off his light, I don't leave his room like I'm supposed to. I linger and curl up on the floor at the foot of his bed and listen to his breathing. I never knew it was possible to care for another being so damn much. I'd do anything for him.

Even risk provoking Jaguar's ire by basking in his presence for as long as I can. When morning rolls around, I finally stand and attempt to tiptoe into the hall.

"Auntie? What are you doing in here?" Franco groggily asks, rubbing his eyes.

"Go back to sleep, sweetheart," I tell him, pressing my lips to his cheek. I coax him into lying down and smooth the covers in place.

Orangish dawn light paints the hallway as I make my escape from Franco's room. Upon returning to the master bedroom, I am alarmed to find Jaguar missing. The bed doesn't look slept in either. Did he perhaps fly in one of his harem girls and spend the night with her?

A part of me hopes so. Another part of me squirms at the thought, and I hate the feeling that washes over me next. Guilt? Fear? I can't decipher it.

I don't want to.

Instead, I enter the closet and grab a clean gray dress in a similar style to the one I'm still wearing. As I shower, Jaguar doesn't pop from the shadows to watch me. I wash and towel off alone. Then I get dressed with an audience of none —minus the hidden camera, of course. I didn't confront him about that revelation last night, but I'm sure he's dying for me to bring it up.

I wouldn't put it past him to be watching right now.

Still, I don't give him much of a show to enjoy. I dry my hair and leave it loose. When I exit the room, Franco is already bounding down the stairs ahead of me, fully dressed.

"Jaguar said he'd teach me to play ball," he excitedly chirps. "Will you watch me?"

"That I did," a guttural voice calls from below. When I peek over the wrought-iron banister, I find Jaguar standing in the foyer, his hair perfectly coifed, his outfit composed of black shorts and a loose-fitting tank. "Unfortunately, your mama has other business to attend to. While we play, she can go over the documents I left for her in my office. It's the room I showed her last night. I've also arranged for her and dear Pedro to have some fun tonight. Now, let's go get you some breakfast. Then we'll head outside and see how well you can dribble."

The two skip off toward the kitchen while I shudder with apprehension. His anger is spicy, much like his nickname for me. It tinges the air and makes my nose wrinkle, even as I rush to follow his vague command.

Down on the basement level, I wander into the empty space beside the game room—only it isn't empty anymore.

I wonder if this is what he busied himself with last night. The boxes have been unpacked, revealing sleek shelves lined with books, a large black desk topped by a computer monitor, and a set of leather chairs, perfect for reading in. Wall-mounted lamps provide ample lighting and create a homey, cozy atmosphere.

Only one personal touch designates this room as Jaguar's alone. A portrait much like the one in his other home hangs on the wall directly across from the desk. His brother Juan.

I gape at it before remembering Jaguar's demand. *Go through documents.*

I find them in a file lying on the computer's keyboard. I steel myself for another grisly bounty listing. Instead, I find information for several boarding schools across the country.

The bastard may be sadistic at times, but his attention to detail is unmatched. He pulled their curriculums. Their amenities. Their schedules and class trip destinations. It seems he gave me everything a mother would need to make a final decision other than the price.

I'm adept in his gruff language to know the unspoken statement behind that move—*Price doesn't matter. It will be covered.*

Adding yet one more debt I owe Julian Domingas.

For Franco's sake, however, I'm willing to make one more exception. I have no other choice. Desperate to ignore my fears, I go through the files before I recall that Franco is with Jaguar alone.

I lurch to my feet, but nudge the keyboard in the process, illuminating the computer screen. What I find there, has me so riveted I can't move—it's another view of the hidden cameras, including one of the outdoors where Franco and Jaguar toss a basketball back and forth. The main difference between this one and the one upstairs?

There is sound. It's low, but crackles through the computer's speakers. Franco's voice, bubbly and high-pitched. Jaguar's patient responses.

If he has that camera rigged for sound, I am sure all of them are.

Including the one near where I spoke to Pedro.

Damn him.

CHAPTER SIX

I refuse to let the horror consume me just yet. Instead, I follow his request to the letter—I read through every school brochure and settle on three that Franco might enjoy. Armed with those options, I finally join him and Franco on the terrace.

They've left their basketball game in favor of sitting by the pool with their feet dangling in the water. Franco is giggling, chattering away about various sports, while Jaguar nods his head, seemingly enthralled. The second I come close enough, he tilts his head my way, missing nothing.

"Look who's decided to join us," Jaguar says, flicking his gaze in my direction.

Rather than decipher the searching glance, I look past him. "Franco, can I speak to you for a moment?"

"Yes!" He bounds to his feet, and I lead him inside to a leather couch in a living room large enough to contain my prior apartment. Seated beside him, I take his tiny hand in mine. Then I sigh.

"Franco, remember what we talked about last night? About starting a new school?"

He nods.

"I want you to look through these and pick the one you like best. I'll be right outside, okay?"

"Okay!" He flips through the brochures while I reluctantly return to the terrace.

Surprisingly, Jaguar is still at the water's edge, but he doesn't react as I come up behind him.

Warily, I break the silence first. "I want to demand something of you."

His only response is to incline his head. "Oh?"

I don't let the chilling reply deter me. "If you truly care about Franco and his happiness, then you'll help me keep him blissfully unaware of anything going on with Braulio. You help me shelter him. As soon as he can be enrolled in a school, you help me get him there. And then after…"

As I trail off, Jaguar claps. "Oh yes. Now we get to the good part—" His laugh cuts me to the bone. Almost as deeply as his piercing stare does a heartbeat later. "Where you tell me what you'll promise the monster in return for bestowing upon you such gifts."

I stiffen, sensing the emotion lurking beneath that statement. He's angry, but I try to ignore it for now.

"You can do whatever you want to me—without involving another person. Not Pedro. Not Franco. Not a baby. You can punish me if you want—"

"Oh, I want." Suddenly, he snatches my hand and brings the fingers to his mouth. With our gazes locked, he kisses the knuckles one by one. Each brush of his lips makes my heart beat faster. "Very much. I think you've found your sole bargaining chip, chica. But what will you use once I take what I'm owed out of that beautiful hide? I'm not sure if you'll have much left to be honest."

I swallow hard. He's right. I have nothing to bargain with. I can only beg. "Just promise me—"

"I am not a child, Lupe," Jaguar warns, releasing my hand. "I don't need you to make me pinky swear and promise to be a good boy. I will uphold my end of our bargain—you should have no doubts about that. But I won't have you scurry away from me without upholding your end. *Claro?*"

"I know," I rasp.

"Good." His lips part into a devious, heart-stopping grin. "What a good girl it seems you can be. Now that we have that unfinished business out of the way, there is something else we need to discuss." His tone switches, heralding an abrupt change of subject. One look at his eyes tells me I'm right even before he says, "*Braulio.* He's gone under the radar, it seems. Even my best men couldn't get a read on him. Do you know what that means?"

I bite my lip to stall having to answer. The truth is, I'm not sure what his sudden disappearance means—for Tiena or me.

"It means," Jaguar soldiers on. "That he is either dead or somewhere safe, plotting against you. We need to ferret him out. I can only think of a handful of ways in which to do that."

"And they are?"

With an expression I can't read, he inspects me from head to toe. "Now, why would I tell you? I think I'd prefer to leave it as a surprise. Just know I will require your assistance to follow through with whatever I eventually decide. Can you do that? Forfeit a fraction of the control you seem so desperate to maintain?"

In an effort to gather my thoughts, I sit beside him and dip my bare feet in the water.

"You're wrong," I tell him softly, choosing to focus on just one part of his accusation. "I am never in control."

"Oh no, *you* are wrong." Taking my hand again, he unfurls the fingers and places them on his thigh. Holding my breath, I read into the gesture far more than I should—the proximity to his cock. The strength coiled in every flexing bit of muscle. The way he seems to relax into my touch as if relishing it. He's trying to convey something through this contact.

Possession?

"You steal every ounce of control you can," he tells me. "You wield it like a weapon, you do. Both a whip and a shield. With such rigid control over your mind, a smart man knows you won't be easily swayed. It takes far more than fear and brutality to get inside this—" He taps my skull with the forefinger of his other hand. Then he smooths the hair back from my face, lingering near my jawline. "You keep your soul locked up tight. Tell me how you met your ex-lover."

I risk turning my face from him to hide how I bite my lip. Does he truly not know? Or is he playing the same word game I was? Lying via omission.

"I was young," I say carefully. "Too young. I didn't know it then, what kind of man he was…"

I hope the vague descriptor is enough, but he isn't satisfied. His grip on me tightens. "And that is?"

Defeated, I sigh. "Dangerous. Unstable. Violent."

"No, not that." Jaguar captures my hand again and brings it to his chest. His heartbeat taunts me through his skin, ruthlessly steady. "What drew you to him romantically, chica? What did he do to hook his talons into your heart?"

Unshed tears prickle my eyes. I never intended to be this vulnerable to him. A part of me wants to run away or provoke him into a petty argument. Anything but give him yet another piece of myself to play with.

"I want to hear it from your mouth," he prods. "I know the rumors. The lies. Tell me how it truly was for you."

"It was…sudden," I say, gazing into the water below. "He had a way of making someone feel as though they were the only other person in the universe. That you were invincible. That he could take your pain away with a smile." *Dios mío.* I hate the nostalgia apparent in my voice. I'm sure even Jaguar can hear it.

"You aren't that sentimental," he scolds, his tone flat. "I want to know what *really* drew you to him."

I shudder at the question, hating the introspection it requires. What drew me to Diego? In essence, it's simple.

"Beside him, I was strong. Someone who couldn't be overlooked. On his arm, I got a taste of power, and I was so damn naïve that I loved it. I craved it. He made me feel like the strong woman I always thought I was. Then he took that woman and locked her inside a cage."

"And you, Lupe, you don't like being trapped," Jaguar says. "I'm sure that riled your feisty spirit. Is that why you left him?"

"No." I shake my head, more troubled than I want to admit. *Dios mío,* this man has a way of dragging the truth out of me. "I didn't fight back against his captivity," I confess. "I endured it. I told myself that it was the least I could do for him, and I let him drain me dry."

Suddenly, Jaguar releases my hand and pushes himself off the ledge, entering the pool fully dressed. Unconcerned by the prospect of ruining his clothing, he propels himself toward the middle of the water, all while crooking a finger for me to follow.

I consider ignoring him, but some impulsive curiosity won't let me. Instead, I copy him, wincing as the cool water laps at the scabs on my back. Swimming is a struggle with the length of this dress. It takes punishing effort to reach him, but in the end, I only traverse the length myself halfway.

He surges the remaining yards to meet me, hooking an arm around my waist. The action presses me against him in a way that makes my breath catch. To maintain some semblance of leverage, I wrap an arm around his neck.

"See what I mean," he murmurs into my ear as if the way my trembling fingers graze the back of his head is proof of his accusations. "I find it hard to believe that you could ever be submissive to anyone. You make this man seem more intriguing than ever, but there is one thing in particular that I want to know."

His hands skim my hips before grasping my ass beneath the water.

"It sounds like he had you on a tight leash. So why the stunts? A fearful woman doesn't jump from a window and demand her enemy come out and face her."

"I wasn't always this way," I confess, leaning into him.

Being out in the water like this does something to me. It feels as though we're miles away from the rest of the world, able to have at least one conversation without our usual dynamic. That's both freeing and terrifying.

"I find that hard to believe," he says, another note of scolding in his voice.

He thinks I'm lying, but I don't shy from the skepticism.

"I wasn't. I would cower and hide in his shadow. I did whatever he asked of me. So, if you were working with him, he could never stomach such outright disrespect. He'd come out and face me."

"Clever girl," Jaguar remarks with a harsh laugh. At the same time, he presses me to him a fraction harder, and my body tingles all over. It's like I'm a horny teenager again, blushing at being the object of a hot boy's attention—only this "boy" has blood on his hands and a capacity for violence matched by very few. "But I do not share my toys, not even my harem women. You have my attention. Let's see what kind of stunts you are compelled to pull off when it comes to keeping my interest."

Do I want to do so, though? I'm not sure. If anything, letting him tire of me seems like a far safer prospect.

"Ah, I can see your devious brain spinning, Lupe," Jaguar scolds. "Don't be hasty just yet. After all, you aren't going anywhere until we get Francisco settled, *sí*?"

Damn him. I hate how quick he is to use my own plans against me. I should take the reminder like the warning it is.

But, *Dios mío*, this man arouses something in me that I can't fight. It's different than the rebellious impulse I feel when it comes to Diego. Julian Domingas makes me...

Playful in a crazy way. Every interaction between us feels like a game of catch with a loaded gun. Which one of us will suffer the inevitable bang?

"It wouldn't take running away or wild stunts to provoke you," I tell him, lacing my fingers together around the back of his head. "You are too calculating to react to such trivial insults. No. A woman would need to do something far more dangerous to make you uncomfortable, Jaguar. She would have to…"

I lean forward and press my forehead to his with a sigh. This should be a mocking display, but I can't deny how good the weightless sensation of being in his arms feels. How much of a relief it is to float and have someone else do the work of keeping me above water for once. I know trusting this man is like trusting a crocodile-shaped "log" drifting along the Nile River. Sooner or later, my mistake will become painfully apparent.

But I can't deny that those few seconds of ignorant bliss are just that. Bliss.

"What?" he prods.

I startle to awareness and find him watching me, hungry for what I might say next.

"She'd have to take advantage of you, but not for your money or power. Emotionally. She'd need you in a way men like you simply aren't available. She would come to you with all her sniveling problems and demand you listen. She'd want intimacy from you far more personal than sex."

I smile, so pleased with myself. Triumph makes me restless. I sink into him more and bring my lips dangerously close to his ear.

"She'd want a partner in you, Julian. She'd be foolish enough to think that her proximity to you meant you cared. Oh, the ways in which she would seek to drain you dry—"

"Try me."

My cocky glee grows cold. I tense. "W-What?"

"Try me." It's his turn to smile, but his eyes display anything but amusement. He's thoughtful, letting his ruthless intelligence peek beneath his narco mask. "I'll be the judge of my woman's 'trivial' problems. So, what would yours be, Lupe?"

He returns his hands to my waist and looks up, forcing penetrating eye contact.

"You've drained my cock more than once, and my patience. Why should any other piece of me be off-limits to you?"

Damn him.

"I'd want your input on my shoes," I simper in a tone I hope is reminiscent of his harem bimbos. "And my pretty dresses. And the purses you would buy for me—"

"Lying doesn't suit you," he snaps. "Neither does dancing around the subject. You aren't the kind of woman to demand my input on any damn thing. Your secrets are far deeper than that. More haunting than that. The kind of dark truths you could only confess to a man like me. That woman? I would let her drain me dry. I would gladly let her pour into me whatever the hell she wanted. Why? Because she would become addicted to the freedom I could give her. Drunk on it. She'd have no choice but to always come back for more."

Shit. He's a more formidable opponent in this arena than I want to give him credit for. Every time I think I can grapple for the upper hand—he effortlessly comes from nowhere to seize it from me.

"I don't think my secrets are of any use to you, Jaguar."

"Oh, I wouldn't say that." His smile widens, and I shudder. "You are very interesting, Lupe. I think your secrets would intrigue me very much. Tell me one. Something you think I don't know."

I think. My heart stutters. I can barely choke out a coherent reply, "I'm cold."

"Then I'll go first," he says without missing a beat. "There is no such thing as love in my world, Lupe, though, like me, I doubt you've had those pretty notions from the outset. There is only possession. Ownership. When I see something I want? I take it. I won't settle for scraps. Do you understand?"

I lick my lips and try to speak. "Yes—"

"You don't," he snaps. "I'd rather you lie to me, than give me a truth you don't trust me with."

He holds my gaze for a second longer. Then he pivots, propelling our bodies toward the ledge of the pool. Once there, he sets me gingerly on the edge, but I don't miss how his nails graze the flesh of my hips until the last possible moment.

"I suggest you go entertain Franco," he says. "I'll be busy tonight. My office is not to be disturbed. *Claro?*"

I scramble to my feet, eager to put as much distance between us as humanly possible. "Crystal," I say, before scurrying to the house. I don't sense my pulse return to normal, even once I'm inside.

CHAPTER SEVEN

After changing into a dry dress, I search the house for Franco, only to find that he isn't in the living room where I left him. Following a hunch, I head toward the basement and find him engrossed in a video game, the school brochures scattered at his feet.

Watching him so enthralled by a fictional world—rather than our nightmarish reality—I don't have the heart to be annoyed with the disobedience. "Have you picked one yet?" I ask, leaning against the doorway.

He makes a noncommittal grunt, fixated on the screen.

The only thing I can do is watch him, hoarding these moments when he's at peace. Who knows when he might feel such again?

So, I let him play for hours with a short break for lunch. Only when he starts to rub his eyes do I gently intervene.

"Why don't we go get some dinner, and then we can go over the schools together?"

He nods and lets me steer him upstairs into the kitchen. With Jaguar occupied, I'm fully prepared to scrounge something for us to eat alone. Instead, Horatio is in the kitchen, manning a stove brimming with several pots and pans. I suspect that he's been commanded to do so by his boss, but with every breath I inhale, I lose some of my lingering paranoia. Whatever he's making, it smells delicious.

"You sit," he tells Franco and me, nodding toward the dining room.

Rather than argue, I comply, and the second we claim opposite sides of the glass table, I slide the brochures over to Franco.

"This one has horses," I tell him, forcing a smile. "And look! This one has a whole science program. I know you love making new things. And this one—"

"Auntie…" His expression wavers, and I reach for him, praying he doesn't cry. I doubt my heart can take it if he does.. "Where is my real mama? And my *papi*?"

"Oh, honey…" I squeeze his hand tight. "They love you very much, but they can't be here right now. They both would understand that keeping you safe is all that matters. I know you must be angry at me—"

"No!" He shakes his head. "I'm scared, Auntie."

I scramble out of my chair and rush to him, holding him tightly in my arms. "I know, honey. I know it's scary here without your parents—"

"No, not that." His bottom lip trembles. "I heard *Papi* talking before he made me leave. He was really angry. He said…"

"It's okay, honey. You can tell me, it's okay."

"He said 'that *puta* will get what's coming to her. I'll kill her.' I think he was talking about Mama," Franco adds in a small voice. "But then he said, 'we'll dump it all. Flood the whole country with it. He can't do anything then.' I don't want to die, Auntie. I can't swim."

Flood the country? Knowing Braulio, I doubt he meant it in a biblical way. Perhaps his product?

"Don't worry, honey," I tell Franco, pressing a kiss to his cheek. "You're safe now. I'll do whatever it takes to keep it that way. Your mama and *papi* have their issues, but they have nothing to do with you. Do you understand?"

He nods, and I snuggle him until Horatio appears, placing two plates of food on the table.

"Eat. Car will come for you in an hour," he says to me.

I stiffen. "A car? Why?"

He gives me an odd look.

"The spa," Franco declares. "Remember?"

Oh, that's right. Jaguar's "gift" evening with Pedro.

As Horatio lumbers off, I'm no less unnerved. What exactly is Jaguar planning for me now?

CHAPTER EIGHT

Franco doesn't need much encouragement to eat Horatio's surprisingly good meal of pasta and salad. Then we patiently review all three potential schools until he tiredly settles on one. After taking him to bed and tucking him in, I leave his room to find Horatio waiting at the base of the stairs.

"How can I be sure that Franco will be safe?" I demand without descending one damn step. A glance around the scowling guard reveals that his master isn't anywhere in sight, leaving poor Horatio as the only one to vent my frustration on.

Unfortunately for me, he is a formidable opponent. Without showing a hint of emotion, he shrugs and heads for the door. "Come."

He's already storming down the front walkway by the time I start to follow. A sleek luxury vehicle is waiting in the round driveway. Inside it sits another passenger, already waiting for me to join him. One look and I nearly trip in my rush to greet him.

"Damn, Pita," Pedro murmurs with a wary glance in Horatio's direction. "All this cloak-and-dagger shit is working on my nerves. I'd kill for an oxy right about now."

He helps me settle onto the seat beside him, smoothing my rumpled skirt into place.

"I'm sorry," I say hoarsely. "I am. I can't believe I've dragged you into this mess."

He laughs. "It's not all bad, sweetheart. I have a penthouse room with a view and a private concierge at my beck and call."

"But you have a knife at your throat," I add.

We both do.

"Cheer up, *puta*," he says with a sigh. "At least we get some free shit out of it, no?"

I can't tell if he's joking or serious. In any case, it's mere minutes before we arrive at an upscale hotel so luxurious I'm sure that renting a room costs the same amount as some small houses.

"Okay, we're alone now, Pita," Pedro says once we're sequestered in a private sauna. Jaguar booked us a full private suite complete with an army of masseuses ready to make us limber from head to toe. Clad in only a towel, Pedro leans back against the tanned wood composing the sauna's interior and props one of his feet on the bench beside him. He stares sternly at me, his dark hair falling into his eyes as he demands, "What the fuck is going on?"

"God, I don't know." I cup my face in my hands and inhale the warm air basting us from all sides. It does little to make me feel any steadier. My heart flutters like a caged bird, desperate to break free. All I can do is lay out the most pressing issues in a way Pedro can understand. "There's this mess with Braulio and Tiena—"

"Speaking of that, I learned something," Pedro interjects, his expression grim. "I had a hunch, so I did some digging. I was planning on telling you all this before Jaguar insisted on my impromptu vacation, but here it is… Tiena cleaned out her bank account, Pita, not even a week before she went missing. A clear-cut cash withdrawal. She must have fucked some banker good to make that happen so quickly."

"Or perhaps, an accountant," I say, picturing the man with whom I'd been held captive in Gatita's cage. An icy chill washes over me as I recall the confusing way he'd looked at me the first time I met him in his office. Like he'd recognized me.

Or, in any case, *Tiena.*

"Whoever she used, the bitch cleaned house," Pedro says. "Bank accounts gone. Credit cards maxed out. She even left her cell phone at Braulio's mansion, but, in spite of all that, I don't think she's dead. She's done this before, remember?" He scoffs when I remain silent.

Of course, I remember the last time Tiena went off the grid. One could say it's becoming a habit of hers.

"I do," Pedro snarls, taking over the narration of this particular tale. "Not even a month after she gave birth to poor Franco, the bitch vanished. Left her own baby screaming in that big house with Braulio."

"I remember," I say, wincing at the memory. Infuriated and enraged, Braulio had called me and demanded I either find Tiena or watch "her screaming fucking brat." I was there for over a month until, one day, Tiena waltzed through the front door, smiling as though she'd been gone for five minutes.

"This is the second time she's left Franco behind," I point out. There goes whatever goodwill I might have still held for her. "I'm sure she heard about the attack on Braulio's safe house, but she hasn't even bothered to check in on her own son."

"That's why he has you, honey," Pedro says. "You're the one who should be his mother. Not her."

"That's what Jaguar seems to think," I croak.

"What do you mean?"

I inhale before blurting in a rush, "I mean, he knows I'm not Tiena, and yet he's still treating me like I'm Franco's mother."

Pedro whistles through his teeth, but it's not quite the horrified reaction I expected. "Well, we know he's smart as hell. Anyone with eyes can see how much you love that little boy."

"Did you learn anything else?" I ask Pedro, shrugging off his comment. I was hoping changing the subject would make me feel better, but I'm more jittery than before. "Like where Tiena might have gone?"

Pedro shakes his head. "You know Tiena. She's craftier than I want to give her credit for. I couldn't find a single fucking trail. Except for the last place she was seen."

"Braulio's?"

"No." He scowls, puzzled, as he says, "it was around a titty bar in Fort Collins. One owned by the Cortez brothers. Nothing special."

I sit forward, racking my brain. "The Cortez brothers?" I know that name, but how?

"Boaz and Bastian," Pedro explains. "They're both fixers, known to work under none other than Jaguar. Maybe your new *papi* is more involved than he's let on."

I shudder at the possibility. "I wouldn't put it past him."

"Well, I hope not. Julian Domingas is a man even I would never fuck with—literally or figuratively. From what I've heard, he has more than earned his fearsome reputation."

"How so?" I lift my head to witness his fearful grimace.

"You remember that big-shot politician guy? Roy Pavalos?"

I do, but vaguely. "I remember the news reports. He was in a car crash or something—"

"That's the official story," Pedro interjects, wagging a finger. "The bastard was running for governor at one point and had the sheriff's office in the palm of his hand. He was a monolith, seemingly too big to fail. Rumor has it, he and his family aimed to cut into Jaguar's territory south of the border—push him out of the cocaine trade in that region completely."

"What happened?" I ask, though I'm sure I already know the answer.

"Flash forward to a year later, Roy Pavalos is dead, his family is in ruins, and Jaguar's empire is still running, even stronger than ever. Word has it, Jaguar's brother is the one who took the old man out—"

"His brother?" I nearly fall off the bench as I sit forward. "Juan?"

Pedro gives me an odd look. "No. My mistake. From what I know, Domino Valenciaga wasn't Jaguar's blood brother per se, but Jaguar liked to dance him around like a little puppet. The nickname of 'brother' caught on."

"A nickname," I echo under my breath. Could this Domino be connected to Navid, the boy who received Juan's heart?

"Tiena may be a selfish bitch, but she doesn't have shit on Jaguar. She just abandons you, but if *he* was your jealous sibling? He'd probably kill you—hey, Pita? You seem shaken up, girl." Pedro raises an eyebrow, his green eyes piercing. "Is there anything else going on?"

Where to begin? I take a deep breath and decide to address the elephant in the room.

"You… You mentioned Diego before." God, I can barely say his name. "Why?"

"Just a hunch," Pedro says, frowning. "Rumors have run rampant about a new player in town who might edge onto Jaguar's turf. Talk like that is always floating around, mind you, but this time it feels different. After everything with Braulio and Tiena, I'm inclined to take them seriously."

Could that "player" be Diego? My skin crawls at the thought and, for once, my sister's drama is more appealing.

"Speaking of Braulio," I say to preface the change in subject, "he's gone into hiding. That's not like him. Poor Franco's worried sick."

And the Braulio I know isn't cautious in the slightest—he's reckless, prone to strutting around like a peacock rather than cowering.

Pedro lifts his shoulders. "He probably knows that Jaguar will filet his ass without a second thought."

"It's more than that. Even Franco seems worried." I tell him what he said to me, and Pedro's eyes go bug-wide.

"Flood—" He wags a finger, clicking his tongue in recognition. "That's a term I've heard thrown around when some small-time gangster wants to push another out of his turf. He lowers his prices and ups his quality to drive the competition out of the market."

It's a likely scenario, more logical than a Biblical flood, at least. "Do you think Braulio would be brave enough to try something like that?"

"I don't know. For Franco's sake, I hope not. Jaguar is the kind of man you should never turn your back on. I warned you about fucking with him in the first place. We're both just lucky you have him pussy-whipped."

"I'm sorry," I say with a heavy sigh. "For dragging you into this. It's all my fault—"

"Enough of that!" Pedro waves me off with a flick of his manicured fingers. "Besides, getting kidnapped has put a few things into perspective. Maybe your paranoia was rubbing off on me, but for the past few days, I've felt jumpy. Like I was being followed or something." He shudders and wraps his arms around his slender chest. "Turns out, I was right, but thank God I've gotten a free penthouse vacation and a spa day out of it. Though, I would rather not find myself—or you and Franco—in the middle of a turf war. Maybe Braulio is stupid enough to make a play for Jaguar's territory. Maybe not. Perhaps you should let Jaguar know anyway. I can tell you're dying to get back to Franco. Go. I can see what else this spa has to offer. Maybe get a massage or body scrub."

"Are you sure?" I'm already starting to stand, holding my towel around me.

Pedro nods. "Go. I'm sure Franco isn't the only reason you want to get back to him. The way he looks at you…" He whistles, sounding both horrified and intrigued. "It's like he wants to eat you up with a fucking spoon. Not even my most deranged clients look at me like that, and I doubt any of them are packing half of what Jaguar is between his legs."

My cheeks flame. "This is inappropriate to discuss," I stammer, heading for the sauna's door.

"Inappropriate, my ass," Pedro scolds as I scamper out. "That man has you dicked down from head to toe, I'm sure. You can dish all about it when we're back in Texas. According to Jaguar, he's sending me back the same day you leave. Plenty of time to enjoy *everything* that man has to offer."

His laughter chases me into the dressing room and even into the car.

CHAPTER NINE

After returning to the mansion, I check on Franco, finding him peacefully asleep with the brochure of his chosen school lying on the floor as if he drifted off while scanning the pictures inside it. As I tuck the booklet into a small pocket hidden within the folds of my dress, I reluctantly leave him and check the master bedroom, finding it empty. On a hunch, I head toward the basement, and as I near Jaguar's office, I hear his voice, low and gruff.

"…get me answers, Gregorio. I'll stay out here for a few more days. Track the bastard down—wait." He sighs, the sound bristling with irritation. "Come in, Lupe. Spying like a child is beneath you."

I hold my head high as I enter his office. He's seated behind the desk, his expression wary.

"I hope you and Pedro enjoyed my gift to you," he says, "I told you to steer clear of this room tonight. You must have a damn good reason to defy me."

I swallow hard. "If you don't want to hear what I have to say, you can deem it irrelevant. Still, I thought it was important enough to share with you."

Though it occurred days ago. I have a sinking suspicion that he might appreciate any insight into Braulio's state of mind.

"I'll call you back," Jaguar grumbles into his cell before stowing it in his pocket. As he threads his fingers together behind his head, I take it as my cue to soldier ahead. "Franco heard Braulio yelling the night he sent him away. He said something about flooding the world. Poor Franco thought he meant literally. That's what I wanted to say. Sorry for interrupting you."

I turn on my heel.

"Wait. Come here."

I look over to find him leaning back in his chair, beckoning me with a crooked finger.

A thrill of anticipation runs down my spine. Is it fear? Or something else that makes my mouth water as I advance toward him, step by step…

"Flood the world? Have a seat and tell me what you think it means."

"Well…" I start to approach one of two chairs positioned before his desk. "I think it—"

"No," he snaps, stopping me as I start to lower myself. "I didn't intend for you to sit there." He nods, making it very clear where he wants me—on his lap.

Easy, Pita. With my chin in the air, I slip around his desk as he leans back, allowing me to perch right over a bulge straining at the front of his jeans.

"His distribution chain," I say, aware of him leaning forward, so his jaw is closer to mine. "Braulio moves his share of product through drug mules that masquerade as door-to-door magazine sellers."

That I know from experience.

"I know he has an alliance with you," I add. "Meant to avoid stepping on your toes, and he cuts you in on his trade—"

"An amiable sixty-forty split," Jaguar says with a feral smile I catch in my peripheral vision. "It's only fair, seeing as how he gets most of his supply from me and supplements the rest with local shitheads who clean their cocaine in their grandma's bathrooms. Everyone is happy. At least until that *pendejo* decided to bribe my accountant into moving my money around. Can you tell me why he would do such a thing?"

"To set you up," I say, voicing the obvious. Then another thought comes to mind. "Or… To distract you. While you're busy dealing with the resulting investigation, you wouldn't be able to properly respond to any imminent changes in the market. And if Braulio could somehow get his hands on another supplier with more product than he normally has, he could release enough, at least in the short-term, to push you out of the market."

In response, Jaguar chuckles, and one of his hands comes around to settle over my thigh. "And he would need a hell of a lot more than door-to-door salesmen with which to do so." He braces his free hand on the arm of the chair. From the corner of my eye, I can't decipher the gaze he casts over me next. "Tell me, Lupe. What would Braulio have to gain by doing this?"

It sounds like an easy enough question. "Power," I say. "Enough power to topple Julian Domingas himself."

"Oh, chica." He shakes his head. "If only it could be so simple. My empire is not quite so fragile, however. Braulio doesn't have the infrastructure to overrun me. To even try would be the action of a desperate, cornered man. Which leads me to suspect that Braulio has been fed a fantasy. A fantasy that would benefit only the bastard pulling his strings. If you were this *pendejo* mastermind, what move might you make next?"

Furrowing my brows, I think it over. "I would have already made it," I say finally. "Braulio wouldn't have been my only target. I would have targeted all your allies. As many as I could."

"Ah…" He strokes his chin. "You would need a hell of a lot of money to do that. And you would need an existing infrastructure to bring in enough product to 'flood the world,' so to speak. I doubt a dumb motherfucker like Braulio would have either. Whoever is pulling his strings must have given him the illusion that he is in charge. They set him up to take the fall."

Damn it, Tiena. Was she working with this mystery opponent?

As much as possible, I try to hide my fear. "So, what now?"

"I never said I would enlighten the woman caring for Braulio's child on my thought process, did I?"

But I need to know. At least for poor Franco's sake.

"Will you kill him?"

Jaguar's eyes flash. "Ah, so that's what this is really about. Are you here to beg for Braulio's life? Should I tell you a cautionary tale?" He flexes his hand against my thigh, his lips tilting in a playful smirk. "There once was a man who dared to cross me. You might have heard of him, in fact. Roy Pavalos, the once glorified patron of our fair corner of Texas."

An icy dread washes over me. Pedro mentioned him, according to the rumors, Domino ended his attempts to weasel into Jaguar's territory—permanently. But…

"He died after a car crash," I say, withholding the rest of Pedro's gossip. I pray my expression seems innocent enough.

Jaguar's cold smile derails that hope. "A pretty tale for the tabloids, yes. Do you want to know how the authorities really recovered him? In pieces. A ploy for sympathy won't sway me."

"What about *Franco*," I rasp. Images of Braulio's face plastered all over the evening news wouldn't bother me one damn bit—but Franco? He would be devastated, and I'm ashamed that reality didn't occur to me until now. "He doesn't deserve to watch his father suffer. It would destroy him. If you do it—"

"*When*," he corrects, his tone lethal.

"When you do it, I only ask that you make it quick. Quiet. Franco's already worried sick because of what he heard your men say. I'm not saying don't take care of your interests. I'm just asking you to help me keep him in the dark for a little longer. Please."

He's a beautiful mixture of stoic and disinterested. "And why would I do a thing like that?"

"Because he likes you," I admit, despite how much it stings. "He likes you enough to be devastated if he ever learned that you hurt his father brutally. He would never forgive you, and he would never forgive me for putting him within your orbit."

"The nerve of this woman," Jaguar says coldly. "I think it's time for you to run along, Lupe. Go give Francisco a kiss goodnight on behalf of his father. Braulio could use the goodwill."

"I am not trying to provoke you," I say, rising to my feet. "I'm speaking with you honestly. Would you rather I simper and lie?"

"I'd rather you not plead the case of a traitor. You care about him so much? Scurry back to him and lead me directly to where the bastard is hiding. At least then, you might make yourself useful. Get out."

My heart sinks. The last time he spoke to me in this way, I found myself inside the cage of a live jaguar, ready to be devoured. My intuition is warning me that I'm on a dangerous precipice. One wrong move, and I'll wind up with the same fate as Braulio. *Think, Pita. Think!*

I want to spare Franco the pain of being caught in the middle of a bloody war, as well as any danger that comes from a bounty on my head. The easiest way to do both would be to remove myself from the equation. Get him somewhere safe, and then draw the crossfire. I don't owe shit to Braulio or Tiena, but I owe it to him. I've been so worried about keeping him safe that I didn't stop to remember that I am not his mother. I don't have the right to make every single decision for him.

So, I face Jaguar and raise my chin.

"You don't need to waste your efforts tracking down Braulio. You can use me."

CHAPTER TEN

"You?" Jaguar laughs, seemingly unconvinced. Still, he sits back, folding his hands together—the thoughtful tilt of his head turns what could be a mocking gesture into a disarming one. In merely a second, I suspect he's sized me up and come to a decision already. Still, he enjoys making me squirm. "So, you mean to tell me that you've known where Braulio has been hiding all this time? *That* would make me very angry, Lupe. I would have to second-guess your usefulness to me."

"No," I say, fighting to keep the terror from my voice. "I don't know where he is, but I can think of a way to draw him out. And perhaps any of your men who might be working with him."

He raises an eyebrow, intrigued. "Go on."

I can't suppress a sigh of relief. One minefield navigated. "You let it be known that I'm in your possession. I'm sure that will send your enemies scurrying from the woodwork."

"And you think that Braulio will come running? He nearly killed you the last time, if I remember correctly."

"You dangled me like a frightened toy then," I snap. "If you want to use me to your advantage, you would showcase me proudly on your arm. Make it known that I am not your prisoner. I am here willingly and have been telling you all I know."

"Oh?" He chuckles, making my heart pound. "But I thought you didn't know anything?"

"I don't. But *Tiena* might. Do you think Braulio suspects she might have seen something she shouldn't have? Or his friends? You should let them think I'm her. After all, to sniff out rats, you bring a cat into the barn and watch them scamper."

"Are you saying the threat of facing me isn't enough?"

"No. I'm saying that if I didn't know you, I'd think what happened with your accountant and a few hiccups in your distribution would have you furious and distracted. You are well aware of the image you portray to the world."

He nods, pleased with that assessment. Then his brows furrow in a way I recognize—he's still interested, for now. Thank God. "So, how can I use you?"

I square my shoulders. "Gather your men and let it slip that you plan to change things. Promotions for some. Demotions for others. Make it seem casual."

Internally, I wince at the plan. It's devious and manipulative, something Diego might have employed to suss out deceit.

"And?" Jaguar prods. "Then what?"

"Then… With Braulio out of the way, you will need to fill his place. And you can see who seems smug and who doesn't. Who trembles in your presence and who remains calm."

"And who thinks they can set a trap for me, be them woman or man. Damn, is that a reckless plan," Jaguar surmises.

"But you will use me as the bait," I clarify. "There will be no risk to you. If he thinks I've told you anything, Braulio will have nothing left to lose. He'll come after me."

And so might Diego. I grimace at the possibility.

"You are creative in your scheming. I will give you that," Jaguar admits. A compliment? Not quite, according to the gleam in his eye. The look he gives me makes my pulse race. It's so damn predatory, seeking out every sensitive area he has access to—my breasts, my throat, even my knees as they press together. "Then again, I think you overestimate your importance, chica. Now run along."

"By the way, Franco chose a school," I add while withdrawing the winning brochure and tossing it onto his desk.

Without waiting for a reply, I turn on my heel and escape the basement like a bat out of hell. My ultimate destination is Franco's room. He's still asleep, snoring, as I quietly take up my usual position at the foot of his bed. Tonight, however, the thoughts weighing on my mind won't let me sleep. When I open my eyes to daylight, it feels like they've been closed for only a few minutes.

There's no point in stalling. After checking on Franco, I slip into the hallway and enter the master bedroom. To my surprise, I find it empty and Jaguar gone. I get dressed in a modest-length black skirt that seems the most casual of the garments he chose for me. Rather than one of the silky tops meant to pair with it, however, I take a risk.

Pivoting on my heel, I turn my attention to Jaguar's clothing. As I appraise the nearest items, an odd realization comes to mind. For all his wealth, his garments are relatively simple, lacking any fancy, expensive fabrics or designer labels Braulio liked to drape himself in. The illusion of grunge must be part of his narco ruse. In fact, the nicest thing he seems to own is a small selection of button-up shirts. I finger a rare white one, amid the sea of black, and pull it on over my naked torso.

In the bathroom, I find an arrangement of toiletries and take my time getting ready. I shampoo my hair, brush my teeth and even scour the drawers for some makeup, finding not even a Chapstick. Apparently, that luxury is reserved for the women in Jaguar's main harem. When I finally emerge and check on Franco, he's just woken up. I help him dress, and we head downstairs to find the kitchen empty.

Here, I take another risk. If Jaguar has grown bored of me, or wants to make a public spectacle of Braulio's demise after all, I'll deal with that later. For now, Franco is my only concern, and I aim to give him as many positive memories as possible.

At least before my actions ruin his innocent childhood forever.

"Are you hungry?" I ask him while scouring the ingredients in a stainless-steel fridge. I'm in luck. There's enough food to whip up something for breakfast without having to beg Horatio or his boss.

Relieved, I set about, picking ingredients for an old childhood favorite I haven't made in forever. While rubbing the last bit of sleep from his eyes, Franco sits on a stool at the center island and watches me.

It isn't long before I sense that he might be suppressing tears instead of merely waking up. He looks sad. I wonder if he had another nightmare. *Damn it.* Rather than ask him, I spin to face him, forcing a smile.

"Remember that song I used to sing you? When you were little, and I wanted you to eat all your veggies?"

"Oh no!" He sighs, burying his face in his hands. "Please, don't, Auntie."

But I do. Loudly and off-key, I recite a silly adaptation of *Feliz Cumpleaños* centered around eating the proper vegetables. I know I'm stalling and avoiding the inevitable. I know that a shitty breakfast and terrible singing aren't enough to make up for what he's lost.

I know that.

I can't stop myself from trying, though, and gradually, Franco begins to grin while heckling me with playful ad-libs of his own.

"We eat our veggies because they…"

"Stink!" Franco interjects.

"Are lovely," I trill. "They make us strong and—"

A shadow catches my peripheral vision, and I break off, whirling to face the man who entered the kitchen unnoticed. *Damn.* He has a way of sucking the air from a room. Despite not sleeping in the master bedroom, he's gone in there at some point to change into a fresh black shirt and pants.

"Morning, Lupe," he greets in a low rasp. He isn't looking at me, and I can't decipher how he feels toward me after our conversation last night. Is he still angry? His smile seems warm enough, though I'm not the one he directs it toward. "Good morning to you, Francisco."

"Morning!" he chirps happily. "Can we go to the park again today? I really want to show you how fast I can run. Can we?"

"Whatever you wish," Jaguar says. He approaches a bowl of fruit on the center island and takes a bite from an apple. As he chews, his eyes cut to me. "I would like to speak to your mama, though. Why don't you go set the table?"

"Okay!" Franco dutifully stands aside as Jaguar grabs a set of plates and cups from a nearby cupboard. Carefully, he carries his bounty into the dining room.

I stiffen in his absence, unsure of how to act. In the meantime, I continue cooking what I have on the stove. Then I hunt for a suitable serving dish, seemingly ignorant of the man behind me.

Until he moves, and I feel his breath fan the back of my neck.

"You didn't wish me a good morning," he scolds. What must be his finger grazes my jawline, flicking a stray piece of hair from my face. "Should I take offense?"

I squirm at the question and use the pretense of rummaging through a nearby drawer to wiggle out of his reach. "Mama?" I shoot back in a low tone. "You want to continue this charade around Franco? Why? You know the truth. Why lie?"

"Oh?" His upper lip quirks into a devious grin. "I don't consider it lying, chica. You are a woman of many talents. Mother. Cook?" He pushes past me for the stove. Without asking, he steals a piece of fried tortilla right from the pan and samples it.

"Chilaquiles," he declares with a rare genuine laugh. "I haven't tasted them since I was a boy."

"I don't think mine will be to your tastes," I counter. "I like them spicy."

"Ah." He laughs again. "You don't say. For all your modesty, Lupe, these are fairly good. I wouldn't have assumed that in between doting on your many lovers you found the time to cook."

I go still, racking my brain to decipher his words. Were they a harmless joke? Or has he done more digging into my past? "If you're hungry, you can join us, though I'm sure you're too busy," I finally say as I transfer the food to the plate and head for the dining room.

To my horror, he follows, right on my heels.

"I wanted you to know that I've made the arrangements for Franco. It took pulling some strings, but he can start school in two days, meaning he should arrive there tomorrow. I've arranged for my private plane to take you both there in the morning."

I nearly drop the steaming platter in my hands. "So soon?"

When I crane my neck to look back, there is no way to read his expression—his eyes are guarded. "It's the best way to keep him sheltered from whatever might happen back in the city," he explains. "Sooner or later, I will need to put out the fires Braulio started. Franco will be far from any resulting violence. Isn't that what you wanted?"

"Yes," I say tightly.

"Good. Then cheer up—" He thumbs my lower lip, and my heart lurches in my chest. I hate how easily he flips some primal switch in my brain. Instantly, my mind turns to noticing everything from his freshly-shaven chin to the faint musk wafting from him. This shirt is too damn thin. Too revealing. Does he even recognize it as his?

Oh yes. Blazing with possession, his gaze dips to my breasts as if he can clearly see how the nipples are already tightening. "I see you've helped yourself to the items in *our* closet," he adds offhandedly, but the hoarseness of his voice has me biting back a groan. Did I catch the narco off guard for once? Maybe that isn't a good thing. His fingers flex as if he's fighting the urge to grab me here and now. By some miracle, he stops himself, reaching up to stroke his chin instead. "I approve of this outfit choice. As for Braulio? His safety, I can't promise. Do you understand?"

"Yes," I say hoarsely. As his calculating mask settles into place, all traces of lust are erased. "Now, I should serve Franco before the food gets cold."

As we round the corner and enter the dining room, Franco has finished setting down the last plate.

"You ready to eat, baby?" I ask with a grin, sensing Jaguar pull back.

Thank God. I hope he leaves. Instead, he takes a seat beside Franco and helps me place the serving dish on the table. As our eyes meet, the bastard winks.

The prospect of breakfast with him feels akin to sunbathing in hell. I'm so nervous I can barely choke down a mouthful of food. I'm too aware of Jaguar watching me, while Franco chatters on gleefully about his new video game or sports.

"...teach me how to play soccer, Mr. Domingas," he suggests, with a pointed glance my way.

Behind him, I see Jaguar's brows furl—he didn't like that. "No need to be so formal," he says, reaching over to ruffle Franco's hair. "You may call me Julian."

"You should eat up, honey!" I lunge for Franco's plate and add another serving of food on top of his half-eaten portion. "The sooner you finish, the sooner we can go pack. Are you excited about starting school? I love the one you picked—"

"Do I have to?" Franco is in full pouting mode, his eyes pleading—but I'm terrified to realize that I'm not the one he's directing his acting toward. "I want to stay here."

"It won't be forever, honey," I blurt before Jaguar can open his mouth. "And I will go with you to help you settle in. Would you like that?"

"I guess," he mumbles. With a sullen, half-hearted sigh, he prods his food. "Will you tell my papa where I am? So, he won't be worried?"

"Of course," I stammer, but my guilt becomes unbearable. Without thinking through the consequences, I decide to swallow another bit of my pride. "Why don't we see if Mr. Domingas will take us somewhere fun, huh? Anywhere you want to go?"

"Yes!" He beams, and I reconcile the small part of me that loathes crawling back to the man a second time. Oblivious to my reluctance, Franco turns his imploring gaze to Jaguar. "Can we?"

Predictably, the man acquiesces to his request with a nod. "Whatever you'd like. I'll tell Horatio to bring the car around, and we can go as soon as you finish eating."

I hate the genuine softness in his voice. As though he truly cares about this boy he barely knows. The same boy whose father he probably plans to gut like a fish.

And I let Franco believe even for a minute that he could trust him.

I'm sick as Jaguar clears the food away, and then we leave the house to find Horatio waiting as expected.

This time, Franco's request is a simple walk, and we find a park in the countryside with beautiful mountainous views. Franco skips ahead, while I try to avoid our constant companion.

As if it would be so easy. He corners me near a ridge as Franco playfully attempts to cross a suspended bridge, squealing with every step.

"I thought about your proposition," Jaguar tells me as I cross onto the bridge and feel it sway beneath me. "The one in which you offer yourself on a silver platter to Braulio and his possible cohorts to draw them out of hiding."

"And?" I ask, eyeing the view rather than risk sneaking a glance at his face.

"I've decided I am not as reluctant to trust you as you are to trust me. After all, you felt comfortable enough to place your son in my care."

My throat grows dry. Did I imagine how his voice thickened over son? *Dios mío,* I hope so.

"Perhaps it's time I extend the same courtesy to you," he adds. "I will bring you with me when I confront those *pendejos* who think they have me by the balls. I will let you do your little song and dance. You will prove your loyalty to me, and in return, I will place a fraction of my trust in you. *Claro?*"

I hesitate. Damn. Spoken out loud, this plan sounds far more dangerous than he's making it seem.

"And what does your trust mean?" I counter.

"It means you won't need to fear anyone, certainly not Braulio." The way he looks at me… I sway on my feet, caught off guard by my own reaction. My chest feels too tight. Do I believe him?

No, but I can't deny that a large part of me wants to.

"We will leave after you settle Franco in his new school. I've made all the arrangements," Jaguar adds, turning his gaze to the boy in question. "I'm interested to see how you work when you aren't preening for a man's affections, Lupe. Show me just how sharp those claws can be."

With a graceful lunge, he surges past me, playfully making the bridge pitch and sway with his bulk. Franco squeals in delight, and Jaguar's booming laughter mingles with his.

"I bet you can't catch me," I hear Franco chirp. A heartbeat later, he's racing away while Jaguar prowls in his wake.

I bite my tongue and try to keep my unease from showing. To my credit, I last until we return to the house for another one of Horatio's meals. Franco is so tired he's practically falling asleep on his plate. Forced to interact with the table's only other occupant, I take my time inspecting my opponent.

Damn him for pairing beauty with danger so expertly. He's in the middle of sampling a devastatingly good tamale, his eyes distant, his expression turned inward. His mind must be occupied by more than just Braulio's threat to his empire. Something personal. In fact, he only looked this serious once before. When I mentioned Juan.

Not for the first time, I wonder what happened to him—and the mother Jaguar bitingly refers to with disdain. Now might not be the best time to broach those topics, but I'm feeling petty after how he cornered me earlier. Besides, if he's sending me back to Texas to die, I might as well take my chance to learn as much about the man as I can.

"You grew up in Mexico?" I blurt out, eyeing him through my lashes. "I'm asking because of your familiarity with chilaquiles."

"Perhaps," he says evasively. "You did. I can hear the accent in your voice. It's faint, but noticeable."

"No. I was born in Texas," I admit. "My parents… They had their issues, and we moved south in a desperate attempt to escape them. I was mainly on the outskirts of Tijuana until I turned eighteen and returned to the States."

I did so by smuggling myself over the border, but I don't want him to know that.

"You have a sister," he adds. "A twin."

"I do," I say thickly. "But she hasn't considered herself that for a long time. To her I'm just an unwanted burden. As far as I'm concerned, it's just Franco and me against the world. And Pedro."

"And you would fight for them?" Jaguar folds his hands before him, inspecting me ruthlessly.

"Yes. They are the only family I need."

"Family." He draws out the word. "I believe you'll find my concept of the term a bit looser than yours. Family is not who you choose. It is who is connected to you by loyalty and by blood. Horatio. He is family."

"And Juan?" I blurt. "What about him?"

"Juan—" Slowly, Jaguar looks up to meet my stare, and I sense a warning bell go off at the back of my mind. "You are very bold to prod something so personal so recklessly." He keeps his tone cordial for Franco's benefit, but my toes curl at the warning.

"Bold and curious," I say softly. "I know what it's like to have a sibling. To be separated from them."

"You insinuated that your sister may have a grudge against you," Jaguar remarks, missing nothing. "Why is that? You don't strike me as the argumentative type. You seem far more likely to cut and run rather than fight."

I shrug off the barely concealed insult. "I... I wasn't there for her when she needed me," I say carefully. In all honesty, I don't blame Tiena. Were I in her shoes, maybe I'd do the same? Trust no one. "Let's just say she probably won't have a picture of me on the walls of her house. Was Juan your only brother?"

Or was the Domino that Pedro mentioned another sibling after all? I'm surprisingly desperate to know. Perhaps the man's talk of family and loyalty above all was just that? Talk. Why the thought irritates me, I have no idea. Watching Jaguar mull over the question enthralls me like nothing else. He could easily take offense, but as his eyes narrow, I sense that, for now anyway, I've wiggled out of any danger unscathed.

"Juan was young and foolish," he says, leaning back in his chair. "A dreamer with no real ambition other than to learn anything he could. To our father, he was an embarrassing disgrace—" he smiles as if he shares that sentiment, but I am not fooled. My stomach cramps in an ominous way. He wants me to believe the nonchalance and avoid going further.

But for the life of me, I can't stop. If he plans to kill me, anyway, asking a few more questions won't change his mind. Danger aside, I want to know.

"And your mother? What was she like?"

He shifts in his chair, his brows knitting together. "She was like any mother, I suppose."

"Did she spoil you both?" At least, that's what I've been told a good mother does. Mine couldn't be bothered to tell Tiena and me apart half the time—and that was when she happened to be sober.

Judging from his frown, Jaguar, it seems, shared a similar upbringing. "No," he says, his tone flat. "To her, Juan was a useful tool to wedge in between herself and those who expected more from a woman with the title of mother." His eyes become heavy-lidded, darkening the brown hue of those haunting irises. "Juan was good and sweet, you see. Therefore, she'd done her job well, or so she wanted the world to believe."

Dios mío, even angry, the man appeals to some sick, twisted curiosity in me. There is something there lurking beneath the surface. A festering grudge waiting to be prodded. For now, I have enough sense to leave it slumbering and gingerly move on to something else.

"You loved him very much," I say next. "Your brother."

"I tolerated him," he replies. "So sentimental. He was weak. Always stumbling in my shadow. A liability—"

"He was all the things you weren't, and you loved him more for it. The master of all the traits you weren't adept at, good and bad. He was family," I add, co-opting his use of past tense. "Of course, you loved him."

Just like how I still love Tiena, in spite of her many flaws. Spying Franco from the corner of my eye, I marvel at him —just an innocent creature in a dangerous world. He's as much a part of my sister as I am, worth protecting at all costs.

"We will do anything for family," I hear myself say. "Even forgive them when we know we shouldn't."

"Family," he echoes me with a low, unnerving chuckle. "And what about *your* family, Lupe?" Suddenly, he leans forward and captures my hand where it rests on the table. Lifting it, he drags a calloused thumb over my palm, sending a thrill down my spine. "Tell me about your sister."

He has that guarded look again, and I'm instantly skeptical. Even though this might be a trap, I decide to repay some of his honesty. "My sister… She was the bright light. The one everyone was always drawn to. The angel who could do no wrong. The prettier one, the funnier one, the charming girl. I resented her for being those things for so long that it makes me sick to think about it. But I still loved her. I always will."

"That's a sad story," Jaguar says, still stroking my hand. Suddenly, he angles his thumb, teasing the flesh with the tip of the nail. "But few would tell it that way. You see, I did my research on Tiena Sanchez and her sister Lupita. Regarding the former, there is a ton of information to be garnered from gossip alone. A feisty chica. Tough as nails. Milked Braulio for every dime he had and supposedly left him high and dry. Many don't speak of her fondly, I can tell you that."

I shoot a wary glance at Franco. His eyes droop as his fork threatens to fall from his grasp onto his plate. I doubt he heard much of that conversation. Still, Jaguar's toying with me for a reason.

Exasperated, I look back at him and nod in the boy's direction. "I don't think this is the time to have this conversation—"

"And Lupita," Jaguar says over me. "She was far harder to pin down. In fact, apart from public records, I could only find a few details. She supposedly died from a gunshot, correct? Somewhere on the outskirts of Tijuana, Mexico."

My blood runs cold. Carefully, I ease my hand from his grasp. "Yes."

"Tiena was already in America then. She left you behind."

"Auntie?" Franco stirs, barely able to keep his eyes open.

"Yes, baby," I say, lunging from my chair. "Poor boy, you're exhausted. Let me take you up to bed."

I scramble toward him and hasten him up the stairs, aware of Jaguar lurking behind, tracking our every move.

Once I get Franco settled, I'm ready to take up my haunt at his bed. A quiet knock on the door, however, robs me of that chance.

Jaguar is there when I open it. With a slight cock of his head, he beckons me into the hall. My fingers tremble as I close the door behind me and step toward him.

"Jaguar, we need to talk—"

"Damn right we do." He lunges, snatching my wrist to drag me into the master bedroom. Once inside, he shoves me toward the bed, and I trip, barely grasping the end of the mattress. "Sit," he commands.

I do so warily, keeping him in my view at all times. I'd been wrong—somehow, I've pushed him over the edge. One errant question had been a step too far.

"What's wrong?" I ask, bracing my hands flat against the mattress.

His lips contort into a lifeless smile, baring his teeth. "You wanted to know about Juan, did you? He was the black sheep of the Domingas clan. The one who drew my father's ire. I was his true heir, capable of continuing the Domingas name. Juan was aimless, with his head always in the clouds. Until one day, he literally embodied that metaphor by falling off a motorcycle going full speed down a dirt road. Splat. Instant brain damage—" He uses his hands to illustrate something smacking against a hard surface. *Bang!*

"They had him hooked up to various machines with a poor prognosis," Jaguar continues, his eyes unfocused, staring at nothing. "He would never wake up, they said. And our father didn't even have the patience to give him a chance. He had them cut out his heart and plant it in some poor bastard rumored to be his. We never did do any conclusive tests." He shrugs and begins to pace, his eyes wild. "That is beside the point. With Juan's heart, Navid became another perfect soldier, and my father was pleased. He had a second stronger, smarter, more loyal son who wouldn't ask the pesky little questions. The bastard was smug as hell about that... Right until I smothered the life from him with my bare hands."

He raises those hands now, curling them around an invisible throat.

"Don't presume we can bond over our tragic pasts, Lupe. That is the kind of man I am. One who kills when threatened and has no shame regarding that fact."

It's the sadistic confession of a dangerous psychopath, and I should heed the warning and then some. I should run.

But…

"You loved Juan," I croak. From what little I know about this man, that love wasn't a fleeting, conditional emotion either. He loved his brother enough to be reminded of him every day. He loved him enough to cherish the battered books he once owned. He loved him so much that even thinking about him riles his rage like nothing else. "I doubt it would matter to you what any doctor said—you would have waited years for him to come back. Decades. No matter the cost, no matter the outcome. You would have waited. Your father stole that from you—"

"Oh, Lupe with the magic tongue," he snaps, whipping his head to face me fully. "You think you know me so well?"

"No," I admit. Not him, but myself.

He comes closer, running his fingers along my chin. "Then explain."

"Your father was selfish," I say, lifting my chin to hold his probing stare. "He stole Juan's future and gave it to someone else, dishonoring Juan's memory. His goodness."

Like how my parents stole Tiena's innocence, but spared me.

"You assume I'm that childish?" Jaguar demands, his jaw tight, eyes midnight.

"It's not childish to want to protect your sibling, even from your parents," I counter.

I sound insane—I know I do. But it's the way I've felt for nearly a decade. Much like the unfortunate Navid, I was also the unworthy recipient of a second chance.

And I squandered it all.

"And you think a few hurt feelings justify murder?" Jaguar prods. He isn't disapproving of my insanity, from what I can tell. His head is angled my way, his body balanced on the tips of his toes. It's as if he's hooked on my every word, waiting for me to give him the answer he craves.

A wholesome, moral one? No. He wants the dark, horrible truth that settles in my stomach like deadweight.

"Not hurt feelings," I say hoarsely. "Betrayal. You couldn't forgive your father for that. If you did hurt him… Jealousy wasn't what would drive a man like you. Loyalty would. You would be protecting Juan the only way you knew how, by honoring his memory before more damage could be done to it. Sometimes… I wish I was that brave, but I wasn't. I failed my sister, and I didn't do anything to stop what happened to her. I live with that pain every day."

God knows I do. "So, if you expect me to be horrified or disgusted, I'm not. You had your reasons. I have mine."

Jaguar's fingers still against my jawline as if he's aiming to test my honesty through feel alone. Slowly, his fingers creep upward, sinking through my hair. Then he yanks a fistful, forcing me to face him.

"Your reasons," he growls, staring down at me. "Like what?"

"Survival. We will do anything for family," I say. "Anything. Even if it makes us seem like monsters. Even if it turns us into one. We will protect what is ours. We can't live any other way."

My eyes burn as I finally trail off and Jaguar releases my hair. As he turns his back to me, I don't care if he believes me or not. I don't care if he intends to use this conversation against me somehow.

Even when he starts to leave the room, I don't care.

Until he stops. Witnessing the way he pivots on his heel is much like watching a fearsome storm unfurl out of nowhere. His eyes flash akin to a lightning strike, his footsteps echoing like thunder as he advances my way too quickly to even blink—let alone run.

His hand shoots out, fisting through my hair again as he brings me into a punishing kiss. I'm forced into an awkward arch as he leans down. Pain shoots up my thigh, but I barely feel it. My sole focus is on the heat of his breath searing through me as our mouths connect—teeth first. A sound like a growl tears from me as he rakes his nails over my scalp, driving his tongue against mine. I have no choice but to relent, and he nips my lip in bruising acknowledgment.

This man triggers a reaction in me unlike anything else. I'm writhing against him, clamping my knees together as a raw heat begins to build in the pit of my belly.

"Fuck," Jaguar rasps, pulling back, leaving me open-mouthed and panting.

The way he looks at me makes my belly flip. It's primal. How a predator eyes its prey before going in for the killing blow. When it comes to me, he uses those calloused hands as his weapon of choice, hooking them beneath my ass to snatch me to him. In a tangle of limbs, we end up on the bed. My thigh is hiked up to his hip as he shoves me beneath him, yanking the gusset of my panties to the side. I can't even process the moment he sinks into me.

Just the sensation of fullness. Completion.

Then, as the bliss floods my limbs, he pulls himself out, cupping his cock. "Look," he commands, his voice so guttural my teeth clench as I feel the vibration down to my core. "This is for me," he declares, as I lower my head to take him in—rock-hard, glistening in our combined lust. "This pleasure is mine. Do you hear me, Lupe? Mine."

Even if I wanted to reply, he doesn't give me a chance. Fingers fisting through my hair, he pins my skull to the mattress and flexes his hips, driving into me so hard the bed slams against the wall in protest.

A cry rips from my throat as I gaze up at him, his lip seized between his teeth, eyes like smoldering coals.

"You feel that?" he grates, reaching between us, his thumb extended. My thighs quiver even before I feel him pressing into my clit, raking a devious nail over the sensitive flesh. "This pleasure? Only I can give you this, chica. Only me."

He rocks his hips as he speaks, ringing a squeal from me. Electricity shoots down my spine, making me jerk, helpless, still bound by his grip on my hair. The bastard isn't lying—this pleasure is sinful, beyond anything I've ever felt.

But I'm not the only one affected by it. A groan rumbles in his chest as my body tightens around him, muscles clamping over him like a vice. Instinct drives me to arch my hips, sending him deeper, and he inhales, his eyelids lowering.

He grinds his pelvis against mine in retaliation, and a chain reaction kicks off. Him slamming into me. Me writhing to assist him. Sweat. Noise. Fire.

We're wild, moving without rhyme or reason—just a primal need to fuck. I don't even recognize the feeling that comes over me. It's senseless. Animalistic. Hunger.

We chase each other up that invisible peak of ecstasy until…

Boom.

My orgasm hits like a freight train, slamming into me from nowhere. Groaning, I claw at his back as he roars out his release seconds later. Utterly spent, he collapses on top of me, and I hate how protective his weight feels, pinning me down. My fingers reach out, seemingly of their own accord, to dance along the black hair growing from his scalp.

I've forgotten, just for a second, how dangerous he truly is. From this position, staring into those fathomless brown eyes, words slip off my tongue before I can stop them. Perilous words. "You are beautiful. Do you know that?"

He didn't. His eyebrows knit together as confusion breaks through his haze of lust. He starts to angle his hips as if retaliating for the change in subject. For trying to reach him in any way beyond primal, mindless sex.

But I'm starting to know Julian Domingas, more than he would like. I can see how deeply my words affect him, penetrating the narco mask he fights to maintain. He's spent so long guarding himself from the outside world.

I doubt he even knows how to handle a genuine compliment.

"I mean it…" My words feather as he shifts, searing friction through my still-trembling core. Already, I can feel him stiffening inside me, ready for another round. Is the bastard inhuman?

Dios mío, the libido he's stoked to life inside me doesn't give a damn. It just wants more. I have to fight for air just to keep my senses as he finally responds to my question.

"Beautiful," he grates, seeming to sense that I won't let this go. "Not exactly the word I like my women to describe me with."

"My life has been harsh and ugly," I say with a sigh as he settles against me, adjusting his weight, so the pressure of his cock is less punishing. More… intimate. He is so damn deep this way. Wide-eyed, I just gape at the ceiling as the sensation of his pulse throbbing in a taunting rhythm resonates throughout my entire body. "I thought you would be too."

And he is. So harsh he orders the execution of others without hesitation. So ugly when he lets his rage spiral into an inferno that consumes him whole. Facets of him are identical to Diego in so many ways, and yet...

The ways in which they differ cannot be denied. I've seen behind his well-constructed mask to the man underneath— admittedly, he's just as terrifying as expected, maybe more so. This iteration of him holds nothing back. Not his lust for me. Not even his future intentions are obscured for once.

After tonight, there is no mistaking it. I'm his.

And he will never let me go.

CHAPTER ELEVEN

Keeping Franco isolated from the coming shitstorm regarding his parents has been my sole goal, but now that the time has come to implement that wish, I'm dreading it. God, I want nothing more than to shelter him, always. Protect him from the harsh reality his parents plunged him into. I hate that he's caught in the middle of their mess.

Above all, I hate that his safety resides on the whims of a man like Jaguar.

Speaking of the devil, he's been unusually tame regarding this whole ordeal. He supposedly had Franco admitted into a private boarding school on short notice, and he arranged for his bags to be packed in brand-new luggage decorated in the cartoon character of his choosing. We're flown to the location of the school in utter luxury, and presented with a private tour by the dean.

Franco is sullen at first. Only after we visit a state-of-the-art sports stadium, and a private game room does he perk up. I stall until the last possible moment before leaving him. He is then peppered with kisses as I promise to call him every night on the cell phone Jaguar gifted him.

Upon leaving, I am resigned to returning to Texas and finding myself once again in a frying pan. Instead, I'm brought to the California house by a silent, watchful Horatio.

"He is not to be disturbed," he tells me before I leave the SUV alone.

Fair enough. Sensing that Jaguar is in his office on the lower level, I keep to the upper floors instead. My heart pangs as I pass Franco's empty room, but I continue forward, into the safer, secluded bedroom I first woke up in.

I haven't forgotten Jaguar's twisted promise—or the retribution he wants to exact against me as a result of my transgressions against him over the past few days.

Why make it easy for him by waiting patiently for the slaughter? My thoughts turn to hiding in the pool and provoking him to come after me.

Curiosity makes me turn on my heel and enter the master bedroom instead. Jaguar isn't there waiting for me, but he didn't intend to completely leave me to my own devices, it seems.

On the bed, in tattered condition, is a small paperback. Hamlet. Knowing Jaguar, this isn't his way of conferring a bit of light reading to me while I wait.

It's a warning. Though I'm vaguely familiar with Hamlet's story, I've never read it. My curiosity eats away at the part of me that knows I should be afraid. Instead, my fingers twitch, aching to delve into the pages and learn what his message to me is.

Caution holds me back. He must be watching me from his office, I think. Although the television is again out of view, and I cannot see him myself, I am sure of it.

A smart woman would hide her fear by feigning ignorance of his presence. I can't. With a sigh, I strip the beautiful, modest dress I wore to see Franco and leave it on the floor. Then I step out of my panties.

Since I assume the camera is positioned toward the bed, I turn my back to it and stretch my limbs, sore from traveling all day. In the end, I climb onto the bed and open the book, not like a prisoner resigned to her fate, but like a devout parishioner eager to learn a new scripture. A novel decree with which to live her life by.

A new fragment of Julian Domingas and his twisted way of thinking.

It is only when I have completely cleared my mind of fear that I can begin to read.

And, *Dios mío*, what a journey he takes me on.

CHAPTER TWELVE

I put all fear aside and focus primarily on the story unfolding in front of me. It has all the hallmarks of what Jaguar's preferred genres must be. Drama. Violence. Tragic romance.

In summary, Hamlet is a man too clever for his own good, driven to destruction in his quest for revenge. Even when it means feigning his own madness, he is adept at shaping how the world views him. He is much like Julian Domingas.

And those foolish enough to love such a man wind up dead.

That is his warning to me. It registers grimly over my psyche, more potent than if he'd threatened my life directly. In the end, Hamlet didn't kill his lover, Ophelia. She took her own life out of despair, unable to understand him or his callous actions.

Jaguar must think I'm the same—weak and easily disposed of.

"You've finished."

The sound of his voice startles me into turning to the doorway. There he stands, his expression unreadable. On second glance, his furrowed brows make him seem wary, like someone who has spent hours pondering some complicated problem without success. Something tells me that work isn't what has him so stumped.

"Did you enjoy your bit of light reading?" he asks me, crossing his arms so that the muscles bulge against his golden skin, making the lines of his tattoos dance and waver.

"Yes, I did," I respond, rolling over without hiding my nakedness. "Your witty sense of humor strikes again, Jaguar. There is just one problem. I can't tell if this—" I hold up the book. "Was a pointed jab at my life or your own."

He laughs, but there is no mirth in it. I jump when he steps forward. He has that predatory intent about him again. Like his Gatita on the prowl. A chase is what he wants.

But I'm not in the mood to give him one.

"I'm ready to face my punishment," I tell him, squaring my chin. "Remind me as to what crimes I'm stood accused of?"

"Cute." His smile widens as he advances another step, coming close enough to capture my chin against his palm. In a rough caress, his thumb teases my lower lip, back and forth. "I bet you repeat that same line to all the *pendejos* who make the mistake of letting you get too close. You pretend to be so eager for their violence?"

Eager, or excited. The same way one might feel after being sentenced to death. In what way has my captor decided to carry out my execution?

"I want something from you," he tells me, continuing to stroke my jaw. "Before I take what I'm owed out of that pretty hide. I want you to answer one question for me, Lupe."

"What?" My stomach flips. Could it be about my past and why I lied for so long?

"How far down that throat can you take me, chica?"

I nearly choke. Some primal part of me reacts to the challenge in his tone, and it's surprisingly easy to form a response.

"As deep as you need me to," I say, refusing to back down.

He steps back, a sly grin playing over his lips. "On your knees. Don't think me sexist. It's a bit of a prerequisite for this type of act."

And it's a way for him to put me in my place. I should play along, unwilling to provoke him. Instead, I stand.

"Given my knowledge of anatomy, I think you might enjoy it more if…" I reach for him, placing a tentative hand on his shoulder to steer him toward the bed. As his eyes narrow, I rush to blurt out, "You sit, and I kneel before you. From this position, you'll have a better view of how good I'm doing."

To my shock, he does sit, spreading his legs wide enough for me to crouch between them. I don't intend to waste this good fortune. I reach for the clasp of his pants, only to have him grasp my hand before I can make contact.

"We will do this your way," he tells me, his voice a sinful rasp. God, I shiver at the way his eyes darken, and I'm close enough to notice the distinctive bulge straining the front of his slacks. Yet, he seems infuriatingly in control. Patient, even. Releasing my hand, he goads me in a rasping voice, "Take your time with me, Lupe. I want you to unwrap me like you would a present. Show me just how slow you can go."

He's taunting me, but some sick part of me isn't insulted in the least. It wants me to take him up on the dare.

Explore him as I would a gift. My fingers shake as I reach for the clasp of his pants with renewed importance. I go slow, fingering an ebony button before sliding it free. Then I drag the loosened material down his hips as he shifts to aid me. Beneath a pair of boxers, his cock springs free, and my breath catches.

It seems unfair for a man who is so dangerous to have such blatant appeal. His attractiveness is yet another weapon in his arsenal, just as devastating as the power he wields to keep his men in line. He aims to control me. Dominate. Subdue.

And I'm tempted to let him.

Viewing him like this makes me hungry for something I can't name. Greedy in a way I've never been. It makes me reckless.

Enough that I eye him through my lashes and whisper, "Tell me what my throat could do to you that other parts of me can't."

He rakes his fingers through my hair, smoothing the strands from my face.

"You should taste the man who owns you, Lupe," he says in a voice that makes my belly quake. "Familiarize yourself with every nuance. Every flavor. I'm the only man who should have that right."

I exhale raggedly. God, he can make something I'd always considered demeaning sound…powerful.

I start to lower my head, unsure of how exactly to approach him. Just use my mouth?

"Wait." He chuckles, continuing to smooth my hair. An unexpectedly hard tug yanks my face up to meet his gaze. "Wait… I want you to look at me. With every inch you can take down that delicate throat. I want to see you."

My head swims at his raspy tone. Maybe I'm just that eager to prove him wrong, but I don't hesitate. I coil my fingers around him, squeezing gently.

"Take me harder than that," Jaguar growls. "I'm not a fragile piece of glass, Lupe. Grip me."

I grasp him tighter. Then I lower my mouth to his tip and engulf it.

"*Sí*, like that." He groans, tipping his head back, all without loosening his grip on my hair. He uses the leverage on my skull to guide me lower, urging me to take more of him. More.

I can't ignore a tendril of apprehension at the thought of taking him down my throat. When he begins to press at the tight opening, I stiffen. I can't possibly…

"Let me in, chica," he says softly. "Trust that I won't hurt you. Trust."

It's a promise that clashes with his prior commitment to punish me. He doesn't strike me as the type to renege on his word. I suspect he's fully emersed in another word game, one I've been slow to pick up on.

Taking my mouth from him, I say, "I don't merely want to pleasure you, Jaguar. I want to *tame* you. Can you show me that?"

"Spicy girl," he says. "Let's see how well you can put that magic tongue to use."

I take him into my mouth again and let him push my head lower. Lower.

He hisses out grated praise while I struggle to keep him in my view. Those beautiful eyes flicker behind fluttering eyelids.

I take more of him, fighting back my gag reflex, even as tears spring to my eyelids. First, a little. Then more, for a second. Two seconds. Even more.

"Fuck."

Our eyes meet though I'm hunched at an awkward angle to make it work. He's so hard I feel him pulsing against the walls of my mouth. It's a struggle not to bite down.

And yet…

The pleasure creeping through my veins feels almost as intense as it did when I rode him amid my twisted fantasy. As though, despite all appearances, I'm the one in control.

Until he takes the reins and shoves himself deeper. So deep I can't breathe. Can't think.

"Damn, chica," he murmurs. "I knew that tongue was magic, but this throat… I think you've found a rival…for that magic pussy."

My brain reels with the praise. I fight the discomfort and take more of him. Until my lungs feel like they'll explode. But this alone can't possibly give him the pleasure that rivals what the other part of my body can offer. I swallow. Suck.

"Christ…" His head rears back, his nails grazing my scalp. "Vicious little viper-kitty."

Drunk off the reaction, I keep going. I take this man in every way I can for as long as possible. His praise dies off, but I must be doing something right. He's thicker than ever, bucking his hips to drive into me at a ruthless rhythm.

Suddenly, his palm flattens over the back of my skull. "How much of me can you truly take down that throat, Lupe?" He rocks into me. Grunts.

And then he shudders, and a dangerous warmth floods my mouth.

Panic shoots through me. I nearly recoil instinctively, eager to spit out the substance. But I don't. I can taste the richness of him in potent form. It shouldn't be so damn nuanced. His taste is different than I would have thought. Not repulsive or disgusting.

It's every bit as addictive as the rest of him.

"Damn." He fists his fingers through my hair to the point of pain. Then, gradually, he loosens his grip, stroking my hair in a way that could almost be described as…caressing.

When I finally withdraw, I do so carefully, wiping at my mouth as I swallow the remainder of him.

"Did I do good?" I ask him, my voice breathless and hoarse.

For once, it seems Jaguar may be speechless. He braces his hands on the mattress beside him and leans back, casting me a long, searching glance.

"Come here."

My heart jumps at his tone.

"I take it that wasn't my punishment," I say, in a clumsy attempt to stall.

He laughs, but the sound borders on a growl. "Come here, Lupe."

I rise from my knees and climb onto the bed. Then, as he nods toward his lap, I mount him. His hands settle over my waist while my bare breasts press against his chest.

"You read what I left for you?" he asks in a deadly soft murmur.

I nod. Just like that, the high from tasting him wears off, making way for the unease left behind by the tale of Hamlet.

"I can't tell if you meant for me to sympathize with Hamlet or Ophelia," I say, picking a neutral topic to bridge the subject.

Or so I think.

His eyes flash, displaying that calculating gleam. "Ophelia was an innocent woman blinded and destroyed by love," he explains. "You, Lupe, don't strike me as such a naïve creature. No. I think you might be more insidious than that."

My heart sinks. At least he waited until Franco was gone to confront me with his wrath. I can be grateful for that. Grateful and terrified.

"Oh?"

"Oh, yes." One of his hands ghosts up my back and sinks into my hair, parting the strands at a leisurely pace. "I think you may be better described as ambitious to a fault, willing to do whatever it takes to further your motives, be it revenge or something else."

"So, I'm Hamlet, then," I say, fighting to keep my voice steady. "Does that mean you are my Ophelia?"

"No," he says coldly. His grip on me tightens, snatching me to him. "It means I'm wondering if parts of you are merely an act you put on for the world's benefit."

"Like how Hamlet faked his madness?" I somehow maintain that playful tone.

Internally, I'm terrified. Does he still think I'm using Franco?

"Exactly that," he says with a slow nod. "Only you fake something far more insulting to me, Lupe. In one breath, you pledge your devotion, but in the next? I see those shifty eyes plotting for the nearest exit. Tell me, why would a woman who claims to belong solely to me, seemingly be ready to run the second she gets the chance?"

Oh. Perhaps this is his way of easing into the more grievous aspects of my offenses. I know better than to brush off his concerns. He wants a real answer. To deny him that would be to misstep over an invisible sheet of fragile glass.

"Because men like you grow bored, Jaguar," I blurt, hating how vulnerable the confession makes me feel. "You grow bored quickly and reliably. The second you do, I won't waste your time by begging or clinging to something we never had. I will leave, out of respect for you—"

"Don't fucking lie." He snatches a fistful of my hair, tugging me closer to him. It stings. My eyes water, and I suppress the urge to pull away. "Don't you *ever* lie to me. My respect? No, that's not what you're after. You're after an opportunity. To go crawling back to your lover the second you sense he might gain the upper hand. That's been your aim from the start, hasn't it?"

Your lover. Not Braulio. My brain goes blank, and I'm silent for too long. His grip on my hair turns just short of painful. He's holding back.

"You never intended to give yourself to me, did you?" he asks with a low laugh. "You merely aim to buy him time. Admit it now, and after what you did with that sweet tongue, I may go easy on you."

"You think I'm working with another man," I say carefully.

His eyes narrow to slits, burning like coals. "I can't think of any other reason you get so cagey when it comes to me, chica. Care to enlighten me?"

There isn't time to come up with a good lie or funny quip to distract him. The only defensive weapon I have is the truth.

"I gave myself wholeheartedly once, without understanding the whims of powerful men," I tell him, my throat tight. "I promised myself that I would never make that mistake again. I didn't lie to you. You have me for as long as you want me, but when you don't—"

"When I don't?" He loosens his grip but holds my gaze. I feel his stare down to the core of my being. Like he's raking over every piece of me at his disposal.

"I don't recall giving you that impression," he says softly. "Perhaps I didn't make my intentions clear before? You could carry my child, should you ask. Say the word, and I'll call my doctor to take that implant from your arm and fill you with my seed tonight. I don't make that offer lightly, Lupe. And yet, you don't do the one thing you promised me you would. You haven't given me your loyalty."

My brain reels with too many chilling realizations that I can't possibly process them all. Not with my throat still raw from taking him and my body at his mercy.

All I can do is fish for a response that isn't faked.

"I've been hurt before," I confess. "It nearly killed me. I think a part of me finds it hard to open myself up again, even if I think I'm ready."

"That's a pretty sad story, Lupe." He drags his knuckles down my cheek, tilting my face for his inspection. "Why don't I believe you?"

"I... I don't know—"

"I'll tell you why." He brings his mouth to my ear and nips at the lobe. "Because I've seen how you love, Lupe. I've felt how you fuck when you drop your guard. Fear isn't what holds you back when it comes to me. Love is. For him. You think I can't see that?"

"I… I don't…" My voice trails off as I stiffen, paralyzed. In this arena, I have no idea what to do next. My usual arguments dissipate.

"I can see him in you, sometimes, your past lover," Jaguar accuses. "When you're too tired or in too much pain to hide it. It's him looking out behind those sexy dark eyes. It's him you cry out for when I'm fucking you. And it was *him* who you were picturing with my cock shoved down your throat just now. Your entire expression is different then," he adds, dragging his nails over my scalp. "You don't have that cocky gleam. For a split second, I can see the real woman, devoted to a man who isn't me."

"You're wrong," I breathe out. "I'm not—"

"I told you what I want from you. Give me that, and you will truly become mine. But if you can't… I am not a man who shares his toys willingly. I told you that once, but I'm not sure you understand what I mean. If you continue to pine for that bastard, I will uphold your promise not to make Braulio's death public. I will save that honor solely for *you*. I'll gut him like a fish, Lupe. Then I'll feed the pieces to my Gatita one by one. I will make you watch. Do you hear me?"

I do, but the heart of his argument chills me to the core more than his threat does.

I'm sure of it now—he knows about Diego.

In that case, he shouldn't see love in me. He should see abject horror.

"And there it is," he says against my throat. His tongue lathes at the flesh before he scrapes that same spot with his teeth. "That look in your eyes. If you want me to believe you, I suggest you do your best to forget him completely. Or I'll have to rethink your usefulness after all, Lupe."

He releases me without warning and moves to stand. Just to stay upright, I have to get on my hands and knees.

"I… I don't know what you're talking about," I insist, though why do I even feel the need to assuage his paranoia? I should encourage any chance that he might lose interest.

But I didn't anticipate the panic I'd feel at the sight of that mocking coldness in his eyes again. I haven't seen it since the night I woke up in Gatita's cage.

When he turns his back to me, I can't stop myself from blurting out, "Wait—"

"Get dressed," he snaps, already halfway across the room. "We leave within the hour. I want you ready to entertain when we land. Show off that spicy little smile."

"Entertain?" I croak, spinning to view him pause in the doorway.

"Yes." His smile is feral, teeth bared. "I've decided to take you up on your offer. We're throwing a little party tonight, Lupe—" He has the gall to wink. "At our Texas villa for all my lieutenants. I want to put your loyalty to the test yet again. We're going to have a hell of a time. Wear something sexy. You don't know who might be watching. Perhaps that lover of yours you've tried so hard to protect?"

He storms into the hall, shouting for Horatio, and I scramble to my feet, unsure what to do.

To buy myself more time to think, I shower first and then enter the closet wrapped only in a towel. At the tail end of Jaguar's deadline, I start to select a plain black dress—but, at the last minute, I pick a red one instead. Boldly designed, it's tight-fitting with a low-cut neckline, something Diego would never let me wear, and far too classy for Tiena's tastes.

Maybe it's my own style, mingled with Jaguar's preferred color. A desperate set of armor against his mind games. I'm terrified to admit that I have no idea what the hell he has planned.

The worst part? Deep down, some twisted sliver of my soul isn't fearful. It's tingling with anticipation.

God help me.

CHAPTER THIRTEEN

Unsurprising, given his wealth, Jaguar owns more than one private jet. We take a model far larger than the intimate plane Franco, and I utilized to drop him off—but there is no mistaking its owner's mark. The spacious interior is a mixture of gray and black, Jaguar's chosen color scheme.

"I'm beginning to sense a pattern," I say with what I hope passes for a playful grin as Jaguar claims a leather seat across the aisle from mine.

I'm rewarded with only a grunt. As he did the first day I met him, he stares right through me, as if our dynamic has reverted back to a twisted game of cat and mouse.

I seethe while staring out my window. Maybe I should keep him bored this time. Let him naturally drift away. I can make a deal with Pedro to maintain Franco's school somehow. The money I have is enough to pay his tuition for the rest of the year—if I use none for myself.

No matter the cost, I should want Jaguar to find a new piece of prey to hunt.

To that aim, I busy myself with texting Franco and Pedro to let them know I'll be in Texas. Franco's reply is only an emoji. Pedro's, however, comes seconds before takeoff—*We need to talk. Important. Call me.*

My heart skips a beat. It isn't like him to be so blunt. Has he figured out Tiena's whereabouts, perhaps? Left with no other choice, I look over at Jaguar.

"Pedro wants me to call him," I say, licking my lips. *Dios mío*, I don't know why I'm so uneasy. My stomach churns in a way I've come to recognize as utter dread. Watching him only makes that unease build. His face is angled away, and I assume he didn't hear me. Again, I try to get his attention. "Do you think you could ask the pilot to—"

"I'm sure *Pedro* can wait until we land," Jaguar snaps without looking up. "I sent him ahead, so he's already in Texas. A few more hours of your time should be easy enough to spare. Think you can suffer me that long without turning to another man?"

Seemingly unconcerned by my presence, he busies himself with something on his lap. I crane my neck to make out a computer tablet. He taps it, scrolling through pages of text as if riveted by whatever they convey. I'm regulated to a mere spectator. An afterthought.

Some petty part of me takes solace in that. He wants to be done with me, then so be it. I think ahead and plot my life with Franco in safety. I'll make Pedro come with us. They are all I need.

"I WANT YOU TO TELL ME SOMETHING," JAGUAR SAYS, A couple hours into our flight.

I shift to face him, startled by his attempt at conversation. Until this point, he's remained stoically silent, pretending I don't exist.

"Yes?"

He sets his tablet aside and runs his thumb along his lower jaw. I recognize the gesture—he's thinking hard, consumed by some mental dilemma. The danger presented by Braulio? Or something else…

"I will only ask you this once," he says, his voice guttural. I bite back a gasp as I feel the words resonate down my spine. He isn't playful or mocking—he's dead serious. "I know that you lied to me about your identity. You had your reasons. We can consider bygones to be bygones, but…"

He inclines his head, fixing me with a penetrating stare.

"I need to know what else you misrepresented in your bid to secure my help." His face is partly in shadow, obscuring the nuances of his expression. Viewed like this, he is a figure more than worthy of the caution Pedro warned me to take, and it hits me now just how out of my depth I truly am.

"What do you mean?" I ask, fighting to keep my voice level. "I was honest about wanting to protect Franco—"

"Ah, not that. I'm referring to the second part of your offer —that you would be mine alone. Was that a lie?"

I say nothing, choosing to decipher his words in silence. I've rarely heard him use that tone. It's cutting and sharp like a whip, slicing through my fragile resolve. I thought I understood my role in this arrangement, but I was wrong.

He isn't bored of me yet—he's frustrated. Resentful. He thinks my heart—and mind—belong to another man. But is he far off?

Yes, I decide, nodding my head. "I wasn't lying," I croak.

For a long time, he observes me, his face still bathed in darkness. "I will hold you to that," he says cryptically. "I am a man who doesn't share. Even if the toy I want was never mine in the first place." He lets that ominous warning hang in the air as goosebumps burst to life over my skin.

Not even a minute later, the pilot announces our descent, robbing me of the chance to ask him more. Once we've disembarked, we're met by Horatio, who flew in the cockpit and exited the plane first. He's waiting near a black SUV that seems overly large for just three people. Inside, Jaguar sits across from me, still engrossed in whatever he's reading on his tablet. Something important, I suspect. Perhaps preparation for whatever he's planning when it comes to this little meeting?

I'm curious despite myself. Rather than question him, I text Pedro to no response. That's not like him. I attempt to call him, but it doesn't go through. Left with no distraction, I stare from the window and watch the city pass by. I never truly took stock of where he lives before, but it's secluded, surrounded by rare swaths of untouched wilderness. It's a beautiful setting in the darkness, especially when his villa appears on the horizon, illuminated with golden light.

A morbid part of me likens the glow to hellfire, awaiting the devil's return.

Said devil exits the car first the second we come to a stop near the front of the house. To my surprise, he reaches back for me, forcing me to put my phone in my purse.

"Lupe?" he asks as I entwine my fingers with his. "*Who* has your attention tonight?" He clips that keyword between his teeth, betraying his irritation.

"P-Pedro." As he tugs me along, my heart races. Together we head up the walkway and enter the villa, which seems worlds apart from the house in California. Near the front door, my nostrils fill with the smell of cheap perfume, and I almost miss the seclusion.

Until Jaguar brings his mouth to my ear. "Smile, chica. I'm sure one of the bastards here is working with Braulio and his puppet master. He'll tell them all about how lovely you look tonight. I take it you wore this ensemble just for that? Were all those texts to *them*?"

"I was speaking with Pedro," I insist, caught off guard by the venom in his tone. "Do you need me to show you?" I reach for my purse, and he smirks with amusement.

"Oh, no. After all, I should *trust* you, chica. *Sí?*" He fingers a spaghetti strap and lets it smack against my skin. My throat goes dry at the subtle demonstration of violence. Something is wrong. During our trip here, his anger hasn't cooled like it normally does. It's merely simmered, growing into a full-blown inferno that scorches my skin with every breath he exhales against me.

"You do look stunning," he adds, nudging me forward. "Picture-fucking-perfect. My guests will drool at the sight of you—and perhaps even some men who aren't in attendance. As you suggested, we'll let them think you are Tiena. For appearances' sake. You should have no problem embodying her personality, I think."

What the hell is that supposed to mean? I'm too chicken to ask. Since the plane, he's been edgy, lacing every word with biting innuendo. Could he be nervous about this dinner?

Or worse—he is taunting me, because all along, this trap hasn't been meant to snare his men alone.

He doesn't care if I'm collateral damage in the aftermath.

As we venture further into the house, my apprehension only grows. It seems he let the party start without us. His luxurious villa brims with activity, and voices of various occupants echo off the walls. As we enter the spacious dining room that overlooks his pool, at least ten men are already seated at the long glass table. The only two places left unclaimed are one at the head of the table and another directly beside it.

Jaguar takes the former, urging me into the remaining chair.

"Good evening, *mi amigos*," he greets his men, who watch his arrival in hushed silence. "I'm glad you all could make it."

I cast a wary glance around, recognizing only a few guests—mainly from rumors. There's Hugo Garcia, a man I once considered going to for help before Jaguar, ironically. Luis Romanos and Leo Corleon, both notorious narcos in their own right, are also in attendance. I'm not sure of their exact role in the trade, but together they've amassed nearly the same fearful reputation as Jaguar himself.

"Gentlemen, say hello to Tiena Sanchez," the crime lord in question declares. A feral smile spreads across his face as he places his hand on my shoulder possessively. "Isn't she beautiful?"

His guests rumble affirmations amongst each other, but I'm not flattered in the slightest. I feel much like I did while trapped in a cage, awaiting his jaguar, Gatita. Like fresh meat.

"We can discuss business later. Now, why don't we enjoy ourselves? Let's eat!" Jaguar claps his hands, ushering in a stream of maids who set the table with various dishes and plenty of wine.

I eat woodenly, tasting nothing, as Jaguar and his men discuss people and places I'm not familiar with. While seemingly cordial, their conversations go over my head, and I wonder if this whole show wasn't put on at their expense but *mine*. Mainly as a warning. A reminder—I am just a shiny distraction on the periphery of these monsters, all of whom seem barely fazed by my presence.

And, in the end, perhaps my suspicions were wrong. None of these assholes were working with Braulio, even if there was a conspiracy fomenting against him. Or…

I'm too in my own head, letting fear and doubt distract me from the assignment at hand. Inhaling deeply, I refocus.

I was right in thinking that most of these men barely spare me any notice—at least at first glance. On second appraisal, however, half of them cast questioning looks in my direction. Not all are the longing, sexual glares of men used to taking any woman they want, either.

Some of them are…cagey.

One man, in particular, draws my notice. He keeps sipping from his wine as if he's desperate to calm his nerves, but I don't sense a jovial mood from him. When his eyes aren't on me, they stray to Jaguar. Then back. Forth. Back.

It's as if he's unsure of our dynamic. Almost as if he thinks I really am Tiena.

"I know that look," Jaguar murmurs into my ear. "Tell me what's running through that mind of yours, Lupe."

I stiffen. Voicing the truth? Out of the question. Thinking fast, I lean over and playfully press my lips to his ear. "Who is the man with the bald head and mustache?"

"So inquisitive tonight." He cups my cheek, making me face him. "That is Boaz Cortez, chica," he explains, softly enough for only me to hear. "A very powerful man. Him and his brother—seated beside him—run an operation known to clean up any 'messes' that might be made in such a business. Why the interest? Have you found your next mark?"

I shrug off the pointed insult. When I glance over, both men in question are staring at me again. I get chills by the way their eyes are narrowed, gazes inquisitive.

"I think they seem more intrigued by my presence here than they should be," I whisper in reply.

Jaguar, however, throws his head back for a booming chuckle.

"Excellent," he says, loudly enough for the whole table to hear. As every head swivels in our direction, Jaguar claps his hands and nods to me. "My friend here thinks we should move this party to somewhere more festive. Who is with me? I give you all free rein of my home, so mingle and enjoy yourselves, gentlemen. After, of course, we get some preliminaries out of the way."

He stands, prompting the men to do the same. The picture of the perfect host, he waits for his guests to exit first, while I hesitate in his shadow, unsure of whether to follow. Suddenly, Jaguar's hand lands on my shoulder, his voice gentle against my ear. "You're invited to this meeting as well, Lupe. Remember to mind your manners. You watch."

Before I can reply, he takes my hand, guiding me from the dining room and down the hall into a larger, more formal version of his office upstairs. There are enough chairs for every guest to claim a comfortable leather chaise while I find myself pulled along by Jaguar and guided onto his lap.

"Shall we begin?" he asks, leaning back, his head cocked at an inquisitive angle. I can feel his posture stiffen beneath me, betraying that he isn't quite as relaxed and carefree as he seems. He's on edge, every bit as alert as I am.

For some reason, knowing that comforts me as his men trade nervous laughter. Only one seems willing to talk first.

"I think I speak for us all when I say that our chatter might bore your guest, *jefe*." I recognize the speaker as Leo Corleon. His dark eyes flit my way before returning to Jaguar, and I can't discern if he believes my false identity or not. "Let her go play with the other pretties you keep."

Murmurs of agreement go up from the crowd, but Jaguar scoffs, his voice harsh against the back of my neck. "I think she's just fine right here—" He settles a hand over my thigh to reinforce that sentiment. "Any objections?"

Corleon scowls but sits back in his seat. No one else objects, verbally anyway. Though Jaguar only allows them five seconds before launching into his "business."

"Good. With that distraction out of the way, we can have a nice long talk, you and I. Specifically… I want to know why none of you motherfuckers thought to inform me about the extracurricular activities of our friend Braulio."

I stiffen at his harsh tone, but—to their credit—his men don't visibly flinch.

"His antics put us all in danger," a man with piercing blue eyes says, his voice harsh. "My men have had to work overtime to cover the gaps in his territory."

"Ah yes, that will need to be properly dealt with, Jorge," Jaguar says. His voice takes on that guttural, authoritative quality only he can master. "As well as why none of you *pendejos* seemed to notice anything odd about our dear friend. I've let you all scurry around in obscurity for now. Pretending that I've been too distracted to notice. Ah, but I miss nothing. Remember that."

All of the men react differently to the accusation, but my attention is fixed squarely on Leo Corleon. He turns the reddest, and once again, his eyes dart to me.

"*Jefe*, if you brought us here as a test of loyalty, you need to look no further than the fact that we all showed. Braulio was a snake. And you should know that anyone around him was just as twisted. Like the woman on your arm, for instance."

"Oh, you've recognized her, then?" Jaguar makes a show of smoothing the hair back from my face. "Tiena here has kept me company these past few days. You wouldn't believe some of the stories she's told me. Though, perhaps you're right, Leo. Why don't you go play with the other girls?" He pats my ass, ushering me unceremoniously from the room.

I obey, smothering any outward signs of irritation. The bastard. He never intended for me to help him discover information regarding his men. He merely aimed to use me as bait. Again.

I know how irrational it is for me to feel angry or disappointed, but I do. Trusting in Jaguar's money is one thing. Putting faith in the man himself? Impossible. He is transactional, focused only on the next enemy on his hit list.

I could always see his shortsightedness as a good thing. Even more proof that I shouldn't believe that he has my best interests at heart.

I try to keep that skepticism at the forefront of my mind as I wander through the maze of hallways and wind up near the pool. Gazing into the water, I feel a sense of helplessness so profound it guts me. God, I wish I could leave this place and return to my shitty apartment. I miss the squalor and obscurity. I miss Pedro with his witty banter.

Pedro…

He still hasn't called me yet to say that he returned to the city okay. Suddenly, hearing from him takes precedence over all else. Without giving a damn as to what Jaguar might think, I go searching for my phone and find my purse near the front door. When I finally fish out the device, I discover a handful of missed calls, all from Pedro. My attempts to call him back result only in a blunt text in response.

Need to talk to you now.

Damn it. Without him as an outlet, I feel so small. So damn weak. I start to find a room to compose myself in—think—but as I head for the staircase, I change my mind.

If Jaguar wants to play this game, I won't curl into a ball and hide.

I'll aim to win.

Pivoting on my heel, I return to the office but find it empty. A raucous burst of noise draws me to the atrium at the center of the villa. There, Jaguar and his men linger around the pool while half-naked bimbos dance in between them.

"Ah, Tiena," Jaguar calls when he sees me. "Come—" He pats his lap in a silent command, but I don't rush to him. It is again Leo Corleon who has my attention. Standing nearest the pool with his back to Jaguar, he doesn't bother to hide the scowl he directs my way.

Interesting. I kick off my heels and saunter to the pool's edge, wetting the hem of my priceless gown as I sit with my feet in the water. From his position on the terrace, Jaguar's eyes narrow, but he doesn't rush to berate me publicly. Even as a blond bimbo slithers his way, he stares past her, his gaze on me.

Forcing a swallow, I turn away from him. Then I wait, and I watch. If Corleon was working with Braulio, I doubt he's the only one. If they suspect Tiena may have known more about their plan than she should have, they'll be anxious to strike. But how?

And will they have Jaguar's blessing should they try?

It's impossible to smother my paranoia. I'm too jumpy. Antsy. Every time I sense Jaguar's gaze flit in my direction, a building curiosity drives me crazy. I can't stop fidgeting and adjusting the straps of my dress. When he runs his tongue along his bottom lip while eyeing my constantly shifting cleavage, I know he has me right where he wants me.

Damn him.

I make a show of smiling and mingling with his nearby bimbos to stall for more time to think. I don't miss, however, that in stark contrast to their giggling counterparts, Jaguar's men remain tense. Whatever transpired in that meeting has them giving their master a wide berth and only pretending to take part in the festivities.

Why?

"Hey—" Someone nudges my shoulder. "He wanted you to have this." I look over to find the blond who'd simpered around Jaguar earlier, offering me a glass of champagne.

"Who?" I ask, though it's not a hard mystery to solve. My eyes go right back to Jaguar, but he isn't watching to see his minion carry out his order. He's being entertained by two other women instead, not that he seems very engaged in their attempts to seduce him. As one of the women tries to sit on his lap, he forces eye contact with me. Those damn dark irises gleam, and he tilts his head as if to say, *Come claim what is yours.*

"Who do you think?" the blond snaps in my ear. "Just hurry up."

"Fine." I snatch the glass and down it in one go. Only as I swallow it down does Jaguar look over. He smiles at me, but there is no mirth in his expression. Whatever transpired in that meeting after I left has him on edge again.

I feel like a rat who hasn't realized she's caught in a maze. My only way out? Confront the captivity head-on rather than go around and around scratching for an exit.

I stand and hunt for Corleon. He's still watching me, seemingly unconcerned by any of the ditzy trappings around him. If he knows Braulio or the real Tiena, I doubt he'd be content to sit and wait, unsure of what I may have told Jaguar about his plan. He'll want to corner me soon enough.

I should stall long enough to make him restless.

It isn't long into my mission that I find myself getting distracted again. Leo Corleon isn't the only man with his eyes on me. While Jaguar seems happy to sit back and watch, I feel like a bleeding piece of prey, hunted by his lieutenants. Just how many of them seek to betray him?

Oddly enough, he doesn't seem in much of a hurry to ferret them out. I meet his gaze and catch him wink. Simultaneously, a hand lands on my shoulder.

"He wants you out front." It's the blond again. She cuts her eyes toward the front of the house. "Now."

I look back at Jaguar skeptically. Just what the hell he's up to? He doesn't think to enlighten me as the seconds tick by.

Instead, he smiles at a simpering bimbo even as I stand and start to follow the blond.

She hurries me through the atrium and inside, toward the foyer. "Just out there," she says, stopping short. With a nod of her chin she urges me along. "Hurry up. He isn't the kind of man who waits."

"For what?" I snap back, but she's already scurrying out of view, her errand completed.

Damn Jaguar. I consider sauntering back to the pool and telling him to go to hell. I even take a step toward the terrace, but I sway and have to brace my hand against the wall. A wave of dizziness hits me all at once. Nerves?

A stubborn bit of rebelliousness makes me square my chin and head for the front door, even as my knees buckle. Jaguar doesn't scare me. I'll face whatever he has in store.

Just as I near the front entryway, someone moves to block my path.

"Where are you going?"

I stiffen at the familiar, guttural voice. Horatio.

"It appears your boss has ordered me outside," I say. "Let me guess? Another…"

I break off as another wave of dizziness nearly knocks me over.

"You stay," Horatio says. "I ask."

He lumbers toward the pool and tells another man in Spanish to watch me.

Suddenly, Jaguar and his sadistic game are the furthest things from my mind. God, it feels like my brain is going to explode. I stumble to the stairs and sit on the bottom step. The world seems to sway and buck beneath me. When I'm wrenched to my feet, I can't tell if it's my lack of balance or…

Someone has their arm around my shoulder, dragging me forward. Then into a pool of darkness and warm, fresh air.

"J-Jaguar…?" My voice comes out slurred and high-pitched.

"Get the bitch in!" someone hisses. They're male but not Jaguar. Their voice is older, raspier.

Alarm shoots down my spine. Something is wrong.

I struggle to regain my balance, but the figure holding me, shoves me forward. Weightless, I land on my knees, tasting blood as my chin smacks off a firm surface. The material beneath me is too soft to be the ground. It's not stable, lurching beneath me and throwing me forward.

"Keep quiet, you little bitch," someone rasps into my ear, a different voice than before.

"Get her blindfolded. We need to move."

Fabric presses over my eyes, blinding me. A heartbeat later, something thin worms into my mouth. A gag.

"Go!" the man beside me shouts. "Hurry up!"

We must be in a van. It lurches again, jostling me against the unseen interior. My stomach churns, and I gag, choking back vomit.

A familiar smell cloys in my nostrils. Cologne? Pedro's…

Is this yet another of Jaguar's tests at my expense?

Before I know for sure, the world goes black.

CHAPTER FOURTEEN

"Wake up, you stupid little bitch!"

Pain jars me to awareness. My jaw is on fire. I'm somewhere bright. The light stings my eyes. I wince, forcing them open. It's so hard to focus…

My thoughts feel like sand through a sieve, and a masculine voice easily scatters them.

"Okay, you little bitch!" A stinging blow knocks me onto my side. A slap? "What did you tell him? Huh? You little cunt—"

"Easy, Boaz," someone scolds. "You remember what that creepy ass *pendejo* said? Keep the damage to a minimum. He wants to watch, after all."

Watch… Jaguar?

The men continue to speak too quickly for me to keep up. "—we need to know what the fuck she's said. If she flipped… Wake up, you stupid *puta*!"

Agony rips across my jaw, drawing a groan from my lips. Through blurred vision, I can finally make out a narrow interior beyond the dark, looming shape of someone lurking nearby. This room is relatively empty, with bare walls and counters. A metal sink…

A kitchen?

I'm lying on something flat. A table? It's hard, unconforming to my body. My hands are tied over my stomach, and the inside of my mouth tastes raw. Salty. Blood.

Another shape flickers in my peripheral vision—a second person. The first stands too far back for me to make out his face, but the other… His voice is familiar.

Damn it, my head feels so damn heavy.

"What did you tell him, you cunt?" he demands, leaning over me, his face above. His breath reeks of alcohol, and his features are surprisingly young. Brown eyes. Curly brown hair. I recognize him as having sat at Jaguar's table, but I can't recall his name. "Where did he take you? Where is the fucker's safe house? Where?"

He snatches my throat, digging his nails in.

"Boaz!" the second man shouts. "Easy. He said we couldn't bruise up his bitch too badly, but… We can toy with her a bit. He never said we couldn't loosen her tongue another way."

He steps into the circle of light, and I strain to take him in. A much older man, with graying black hair and piercing blue eyes. Him, I know as well. Bastian Cortez. The other must be his brother Boaz.

"Look at me, mamacita," Bastian croons. A warm pressure settles over my thigh, creeping upward. My breath catches as I recognize the touch for what it is—fingers.

Oh, God.

"Be good to us, and we can keep this encounter short and sweet, yes? A friend of ours wants us to ask you some questions. Be truthful, and we'll let you go. Now, tell us about where you went with *El Jaguar*."

Jaguar. His name awakens the skeptical part of my brain. Ah, so *this* must be his trick. Why he was so damn smug. Torture is the game he wants to play to test my loyalty to him—so much so that his goons don't even try to disguise his role. They stupidly let it slip that he's watching this from afar, desperate to see me break.

And I am so damn tempted to. I open my mouth to tell Jaguar exactly what I know about him. That he is a bastard. A liar. A fucking fool.

Then I remember…

I'd be playing right into his hands, proving his twisted suspicion correct. He wants loyalty? Oh, I'll show him loyalty.

Wrestling control over my tongue, I face Bastian Cortez. My mouth is so dry I can barely choke out, "Go to hell."

"Bitch—" His brother seizes a fistful of my hair, wrenching my face toward him. "Where did he take you?"

I say nothing.

"I think she needs more fucking convincing," Boaz snarls, releasing me. "I don't think your methods are working, *cabrón.*"

"Oh, they will work."

Bastian steps into view as I feel his fingers creep higher, inching beneath the skirt of my dress.

Oh, God. I try to breathe. Think. Do anything but scream. A frightened whimper drips out of me anyway as one pathetic thought circles my brain. *How could he?*

All this time, I'd convinced myself that I didn't trust Jaguar further than I could throw him—but it was a lie. I'd naïvely thought him incapable of this—cold, brutal evil. How could a man who claimed to want me to bear his children, let one of his bastards violate me in the next breath? The rage from betrayal rips through me, and I feed off it. I cling to it. It's all I have.

Even as Bastian shoves a finger inside me, I breathe.

"I won't tell you a damn thing. You think this can break my loyalty to him?" I force out a laugh that becomes a double-edged sword as tears fall from my eyes to undermine it. "Do what you will. You know he's watching."

"Don't listen to this stupid bitch," Boaz snarls. His shoulder flexes, and then…black! Pain rips through my skull, and I hear my cry echoing weakly off the walls. "Tell us where the fuck he took you! Where is the safe house?"

I picture the house in California. It must be important to him if he tasked his men with trying to beat it out of me. A new property, perhaps? One purchased off the grid. He drugged me to bring me there, but not when I left.

The mystique, I suspect, is all part of his test.

"I don't know what you're talking about," I lie. "Ask Jaguar himself."

Another finger is shoved into me beside the first, and my resolve breaks. I can't endure more of this—I can't. It shatters me, ripping me back to my past as a frightened little girl, forcing herself to turn violence into affection.

I try to focus on hate. I let it ground me enough that I can ignore any damage done to my body. It's the emotion that saved me from Diego, and I welcome it as a useful tool against Jaguar.

"You're wasting your time," I tell them, hating how hoarse my voice sounds. How broken. "Pain alone won't shake my loyalty to him. You'll just have to kill me."

"I say we take her up on that offer," Boaz snarls. His hands go around my throat again, squeezing so hard I see stars. Bound as I am, all I can do is flail, unable to fight. Scream.

Gradually, my vision blurs, though I doubt he'll truly kill me. But if I lose consciousness, who knows what they'll do to my body in the meantime…

Fight, Pita. Fight!

Suddenly air! I gasp a lungful as the pressure on my neck loosens, and Boaz recoils. But something is wrong. There's water dripping onto me from somewhere. Wet, warm water…

A thud echoes from nearby, and a voice calls out, followed by a loud pop. Then a groan. And silence, broken only by a familiar voice that drips into my ear.

"Can you hear me, Lupe?"

I barely can.

Only because I can't stop screaming.

CHAPTER FIFTEEN

I've never wished for death, even during the worst depths of my relationship with Diego. I still don't. I'm just prideful. After going so long without letting myself fall under the spell of another man, my battered psyche stings. I'd give anything to not feel so broken ever again.

I crave the fragile stability I had just a few days ago when Franco was my only concern. I'd sell my soul to get that back... And I'd give up far more to put as much distance as possible between me and the man I find when I peel my sore, aching eyes open.

He's seated beside me on what must be a bed. I recognize his masculine scent, and it, paired with the eerie gentleness of the fingers raking through my hair, helps paint a mental image.

"I can smell the anger on you, chica," he says softly, continuing to stroke my scalp. "You are safe now, but

Horatio had to drug you. You were in no state to be moved otherwise. You were hysterical."

I wait to hear the typical mocking tone that infects his voice. I wait for him to deliver some cruel praise for surviving his trick. I wait.

"It is not often that I admit when I was wrong," he adds, in a tone much deeper than what I'm used to. There is no taunting in it, still. Just the low, raspy hum of a predator capable of untold violence—but, for whatever reason, he's keeping himself restrained. "Once again, I underestimated what my men will do in your presence. They were wild dogs, spooked by the bastard pulling their leash—who, in this instance, wasn't me. I will not rest until I find out who."

My heart pangs. This isn't right. He should be gloating, not...

Confessing?

"You should know that Pedro is missing."

He says it so tonelessly that it takes my brain a second to process. *No.* I heard him wrong. Voice breaking, I try to speak. "What—"

"It seems he didn't leave the airport after arriving in Texas," Jaguar continues over me. "They must have ambushed him there and used his phone to contact you."

He waits—letting it sink in, I think. Waiting for me to scream and cry and put on theatrics. A part of me wants to. My eyes are already watering, my throat so tight it hurts to breathe, but I don't sob or wail. Pedro deserves more than that.

He deserves more than me as a friend. "You need to find him!"

"I will," Jaguar says with a nod. "This was sent to your cell phone not long ago."

He holds up the device for me to see.

"Oh, God."

Pedro kneels before a black backdrop that obscures his surroundings. Blood is smeared across his lower lip, but apart from that, he's alive, his eyes fixed on the camera.

"My Butterfly," he says, but his voice is monotone. Wide with fear, his eyes dart from the camera's lens to a space just left of it. He must be reading off something. "If you want him back, come and get him. He won't be harmed before then. Take your time, knowing that with every delay, I'll adjust your punishment."

The video goes dead.

"It was being broadcast from another location," Jaguar adds. "Along with their video of you. Boaz can no longer cause you harm, but Bastian... He awaits his final judgment at your discretion."

"I don't care about revenge," I manage to spit. "I need Pedro. God, he could be…"

Tortured. Mutilated. Dead—because of me. Even at the hint of Diego's return, I should have done something. I should have protected him.

As if to taunt me, a familiar mocking voice echoes in my mind, *Did you think I would let you go so easily, Butterfly? Hell no. You will pay…*

"You're angry, but you aren't a fool. Dealing with Bastian Cortez isn't a mercy," Jaguar explains as his hand stills against my cheek. "This isn't even a gift. It is the right you earned. You defended me against that *pendejo,* and for that, you earned a say in how he is punished. That is the least of what you have earned after tonight. If he knows anything about Pedro's whereabouts, I will discover it. But worrying yourself sick won't help him now. You're smarter than that."

He stands, putting his back to me. I can sense a heaviness in his posture that isn't normally there. A quiet, stoic rage, and unyielding strength. He's dropped his mask again, letting me glimpse the real Julian Domingas beneath.

And for a second, just one, I consider that he wasn't behind the attack after all. It caught even him off guard—but the prospect of him being outplayed is more terrifying than one of his mind games.

"First, you need rest," Jaguar continues. "I'm sending you back to our home tonight—"

"No." I try to sit up. "I'm not leaving—"

"It's yours, paid for in blood," he continues as if I never spoke. "A doctor will meet you there to deal with your injuries. Horatio will accompany you, and I will join you shortly *with* information on Pedro. Then, I'll face the wrath in those eyes, chica. I deserve it for failing to honor the trust you have placed in me, but know this... The time for play is over. You are mine."

He leaves what I slowly recognize as the private suite in his manor. Not long after, Horatio enters, with a black duffle draped over one arm.

"We leave tonight," he tells me in a brusque tone. "No phone. You will get a new one when we land."

"Wait." I attempt to sit upright. "I'm not going anywhere. Not until I know that Pedro—"

"You leave tonight." Horatio steps forward as if to help me to my feet, but I beat him to the punch, moaning with every muscle I have to flex to stand. I'm shaking. My knees buckle, and I nearly fall when I try to take a step.

Somehow, though, I remain standing.

No matter what life, or Jaguar or even Diego, throws at me...I will always remain standing.

CHAPTER SIXTEEN

I t kills me to admit it, but Jaguar was right—panicking over Pedro will get me nowhere. Right now, my old friend needs far more from me than self-pity. Besides, giving into fear would only be playing into Diego's hands in the long run. As painful as it is to watch the minutes tick by, I must think clearly.

At least there is one small shred of hope to take comfort in. I know Diego. If he did take Pedro, he'd keep him alive—long enough to make me come crawling to him on my hands and knees.

Trusting Jaguar in the short-term is the only option to circumvent him. In any case, the narco has stayed true to his word. I'm ushered onto his private plane by Horatio and transported in utter luxury. When Horatio drives me to my final destination in a private car, I am not surprised.

Bathed in the blood-red glow of sunset, Jaguar's modern mansion in the California hills cuts a striking image. At first glance, I'm not sure whether to feel relieved or doomed.

With little fanfare, Horatio parks in the driveway and escorts me inside.

"The doctor is waiting upstairs," he warns to preface the arrival of the stern-faced brunette I met once before in Jaguar's villa. She ushers me into the empty bedroom and commences a succinct inspection of my scratches and bruises. In the end, her only prescription is for rest with the aid of a sleeping medication she leaves on the nightstand. As soon she exits the room for good, every ounce of guilt I had suppressed until then comes rushing back. I start to follow her, only to change course and wind up in the bathroom attached to Franco's room. If I breathe in deeply enough, I swear I can still smell him, though all other traces of his presence are gone.

The pathetic woman I am, I hoard every memory I can and huddle in the bath where I washed him just days ago. There, I forget my promise to myself. I don't pick up the pieces and remain stoically behind my armor.

I just sink beneath the water, letting it rise until my entire body is submerged. I wait until my lungs burn before I come up for air. The second I do, I hear a knock on the door.

"*Señora.* Is everything okay?" The voice is Horatio's.

I don't put it past him to break down the door if I don't respond quickly enough. Not out of concern for me, but loyalty to his boss. No matter what, he will protect Jaguar's investment.

The sobering thought snaps some sense back into me. "I'm fine," I call out. With a sigh, I climb from the tub and step into a towel. Dripping wet, I leave Franco's room—thankfully, without running into Horatio—and pad down the hall into the room Jaguar and I shared.

More than a few things have changed since my last visit. For one, "our" bed has been modified, with a thicker set of blankets placed atop the black sheets. One side has been drawn back, with a black silk sleeping mask resting on the pillow, presumably on the side I'm meant to claim.

And that isn't all.

Jaguar has already upheld one promise to me—a new phone is waiting for me at the foot of the bed. Alongside it is a replacement for my purse—only instead of the knockoff one I borrowed from Pedro, this black leather bag looks real. Real designer. Real fucking expensive, too. Warily, I peek inside it before turning my attention to the other "gifts" Jaguar had left for me to find.

Alongside the phone is my passport—*mine*, not Tiena's, along with a driver's license and an object that makes me do a double take. It resembles the car keys Pedro likes to wave around. The kind meant for a very expensive car, in fact. For now, I shove them inside the purse.

The phone itself has only two numbers programmed into it. One is for Franco, and I can't silence a sob of relief. The other number, however, undercuts any gratitude I may feel.

Julian. This intimate detail puts me on guard, and a warning bell rings in my head.

To compound my growing unease, the phone rings as if he's watching me from afar, waiting for this exact moment.

With a sigh, I answer.

"You received my gifts," a low voice states. "There is more. When I join you, I will give the bulk to you then. In the meantime, we have reason to believe Pedro is still alive. My men are still tracking down his whereabouts."

"Thank God," I breathe out. "But how do you know?"

There are a few seconds of silence. Hesitation on his part? Then, "I will explain in person."

I can't hide my frustration. "So, you expect me to just sit around twiddling my thumbs until then?"

"No. I expect you to fully discover everything I left for you," he says, eerily calm.

More money. More designer purses, I suspect. More Band-Aids to plaster over the damage he's done. The sad part?

I don't know how to react to them. Diego never apologized to me with gifts. I was weak enough to forgive him outright, even when he didn't ask.

"I would be a fool to stay here. You lied to me, Jaguar," I hear myself say in a voice I don't recognize. "You… You let those men hurt me. You watched them do it."

A reply doesn't come, but I can hear him breathing into the phone. Then the line goes dead, and maybe some small part of me is grateful for the sudden disconnect. It means he chose not to lie. Not to deny.

Ironically, it's a small shred of dignity Diego never gave me. And it makes it even easier for me to resent the man standing in his place.

I set the phone aside, and lie back, though I know better than to even try to sleep.

After a fruitless few seconds of tossing and turning, I get up. If Jaguar's loyalty means offering me on a platter to be abused by his enemies, then his concept of privacy means nothing. Head held high, I dress blindly in a shirt from his closet and head downstairs. As I near the bottom step, Horatio appears seemingly from nowhere.

"He wants you to rest," he insists, his expression blank. "Until he comes back."

I ignore him and push past him into the basement. When I reach the room designated as Jaguar's office, I half expect to find it empty, devoid of any secrets I could parse through in his absence. Instead, the door isn't locked, and it contains the items I remember. Bookshelves, a desk, and a computer.

As I scan the room, what he said on the phone finally clicks —even here, it seems he left some gifts for me. There is a stack of files on the desk. Horatio doesn't seem surprised by their presence, and when I reach for the topmost folder, he merely sighs in disapproval.

"He wanted you to rest first," he explains in a scolding tone. "You better understand then."

Bullshit.

"Like Pedro understands why he's suffering because of me?" Without expecting a response, I sit in the nearest chair and boldly flip open the file. The documents I find within cool my rebellious rage.

It's a dossier entirely devoted to Leo Corleon, but far more comprehensive than a broad-strokes outline I could glean on my own, containing information about his family, his known aliases and safe houses, and even his businesses. Hints to his true occupation as a gambling magnate with ties to money laundering pepper the detailed records. All in all, they provide an in-depth view of the man in nearly every aspect.

Almost as if…

Jaguar had it prepared for me.

My fingers shake as I reach for another file and find a similar info dump on Hugo Garcia. Then Kique Gomez. The Cortez brothers.

By the time I finish, I count twelve files—one for each of the eleven men Jaguar had at his little house party the other night. And, of course, one extra to account for Braulio Rivera.

With reluctant interest, I work my way through the Cortez brothers first. I'm halfway through the one on Boaz when Horatio shifts, noisily rummaging through his pockets. All this time, he's been watching me from the doorway without saying a word.

I look over to find him frowning—a rare display of emotion—as he brings a cell phone to his ear. "*Sí?* You weren't expected back for two days, *señor*," he says, his voice both gruff and deferential. "I understand, but the precautions… *Sí*, I'll arrange it. Yes, *señor*." He hangs up.

The fact that he let me overhear that conversation at all betrays some deliberateness on his part. I'm sure of that much, even before he meets my stare head-on and says, "Mr. Jaguar will return tonight."

I swallow, not knowing how to interpret that statement. As a threat?

Pushing the thought from my mind, I return to my current task and study each and every last one of Jaguar's men. With every new file devoured, I have a better grasp of the internal dynamics that make Jaguar's empire seem less like a well-oiled machine, and more like a well-crafted house of cards—only the cards have razor blades embedded in their edges.

One wrong move, and the entire thing topples.

Jaguar, at the center of them all, seems to have carefully arranged his lieutenants in a hierarchy that displays a twisted, intimate knowledge of the human psyche. He knows their every weakness. What makes them tick. Their susceptibilities to blackmail. Their desires. I'm sure he felt he could control these men implicitly, no matter the outside threat.

Until now. The Cortez brothers chose to betray him, and a new, unknown variable has come into play. I have a grim suspicion as to what that might be—or who… These men are beholden to a new monster they fear more than Jaguar himself.

Even Jaguar, with all his cunning and intelligence, didn't see that coming.

The second I set aside the last file, Horatio withdraws his phone again. "*Sí. Claro,*" he says into the receiver before returning his attention to me. "Mr. Jaguar is arriving now."

I marvel at the time that must have passed. A few hours, at least. Almost as if during our phone call, he was either on his way to the airport, or left right after.

No doubt to greet his master, Horatio retreats with a sigh, but I don't move. Instead, I dump the files haphazardly on the desk and wait. After only a few seconds, I can sense the quiet commotion caused by Jaguar's arrival.

Several sets of footsteps echo throughout the upstairs, betraying the presence of more than one person. This time, perhaps he brought an entourage? No. These footsteps are too heavy and stern, resonating like the uniformed soldiers who march along the border. Brusque, efficient, and focused on their task.

A shudder runs down my spine. Perhaps he brought reinforcements to torture more answers out of me? I don't seriously consider the possibility until those efficient footsteps head into the basement.

Right in my direction.

With wide eyes on the doorway, I see Jaguar first. Standing tall, he storms past the office, and I catch a glimpse of the men he brought with him. I was right—they aren't the giggling bimbos and snickering *pendejos* he usually surrounds himself with. Four men in black drag a large metal case between them.

My brain brims with suspicions as to what might be inside it. Did Jaguar decide to bring his precious Gatita here?

Well, I don't plan on sticking around to find out. Rising to my feet, I start to head upstairs, as far from him as the house will allow.

I hear his voice the moment I enter the hall. "Lupe."

My feet twitch against the floor as I consider running. In the end, pride roots me in place as I pivot to look over my shoulder. *Dios mío.* Despite everything this man has put me through, my belly clenches at the sight of him. He stands at the other end of the hallway, beside a set of closed doors I have yet to venture through. Like his new friends, he's dressed in a black button-down shirt and a pair of slacks. The ensemble reflects the narco kingpin he truly is. Sometimes he's so good at playing the role of mindless brute, I almost forget the calculating figure lurking behind the mask.

The way he looks at me now is how I assume he eyes all of his potential conquests—eyes narrowed, jaw clenched. Without warning, he surges forward, and I instinctively back into the room I just left.

Jaguar is undeterred, looming in the doorway. "You want your answers?" he asks, his tone level. "Then come." He turns and heads back the way he came while I watch him from the doorway. His arrival serves as a painful reminder of everything that's happened. Franco leaving. Pedro. The Cortez brothers…

I can still feel their filthy hands on me, and I wrap my arms around my front to dispel the feeling. *Dios mío*, I hate being so weak. So pathetic.

"You aren't the jumpy type, Lupe," Jaguar remarks. I didn't realize he'd spun to face me again. His advancing footsteps resonate down to my bones, and I give in to the childish urge to run, skirting the desk in his office to brace myself against one of the bookshelves at the far wall.

"Get away from me," I hiss as he slips into the room, his head lowered, eyes obscured.

"Ah," he says softly. "So, you aren't just gifted with a magic tongue. You hold grudges, too. Grudges against the men who you believe have wronged you. Will you add me to your list?"

I bristle at the caution in his tone. It's more irritating than his smug, mocking laughs. As if he really cares that he might have upset me.

Like hell, will I fall for that trick.

"I will add you to the same list that I add the men who want to use me only to their own ends. It's rather long, so you have company there," I spit. "The only thing I want from you is to find Pedro or get the hell out of my way."

"Look at me."

I spin around to put my back to him, eyeing the spines of the books nearest me. There are volumes of Shakespeare interspersed with encyclopedias and tomes on various topics. I finger one and try to ignore the alarm running down my spine as I sense him come up behind me.

"You make it rather difficult to apologize," he says. "Almost as if you're not used to it. I could hear the anger in your voice earlier. When my woman is upset, not even my business takes precedence over her. I got on a plane ten minutes after."

Is that true? Horatio certainly seemed annoyed by the change in Jaguar's arrival. I mull over the prospect of him rushing back just for me as his breath fans the back of my neck. Radiating possession, his hand grazes my hip next, the fingers outstretched.

I try to shift out of his reach, gripping the nearest shelf for balance. "Is that what you're doing right now, Jaguar?" I rasp out. "Apologizing?"

I'm feeling bitter enough to twist the knife, even as my heart races when his fingers rake through my hair next.

"Shouldn't a man get down on one knee, with flowers and chocolates?"

As if I know a damn thing about such gestures. Diego never apologized—and he certainly wouldn't fly halfway across the country to address my concerns in person. Neither did my parents feel remorse for the hell they put my sister and me through. A man like Jaguar most definitely doesn't.

"Real men do far more than that, chica," he says softly. "But you wouldn't know that. You think I doubted you. That makes you angry—you have a right to be. You know to take offense when the man meant to protect you has forsaken his vow. You know your worth. But..." He's closer, his voice dripping into my ear. "Give me a chance to show you how a real man apologizes to his woman before you pass judgment, *sí?*"

He takes my hand, tugging me into him. My arms go around his waist out of sheer force of a habit. The resulting embrace is too fleeting to be called a hug. It's more like... A full body caress. Perhaps his way of issuing yet another apology before he turns and guides me from the room. I shiver, feeling my heart pound like mad as his heat slams into me like a battering ram. I can feel the muscles of his chest flexing against my back as he leads me into the hall and toward those closed double doors.

The second we draw near, they part from the inside, revealing a wide, open space enclosed by gray walls and concrete flooring. Digging my heels in, I remember the horrifying moment when I woke up in Gatita's cage.

"It's alright." Jaguar tugs on my hand, wrenching me forward. Only then do I realize that this room lacks a characteristic animal musk, and there is no jaguar in sight. Something strange, however, is lying on its side in the middle of the concrete floor. I strain to identify it. A mannequin with splayed limbs, splattered in red…?

"This is my first act of atonement to you," Jaguar explains before I've identified the shadowy mass fully. I feel him release my hand as he steps forward, and another overhead light switches on.

As my eyes adjust to the dim lighting, I note the four men in black lurking on the outskirts of the room. A table against the far wall has a series of objects that I can't make out clearly.

Not until Jaguar approaches and removes something from the array, lifting it for me to see. My breath catches, and my hands start to sweat. He's decided to forgo feeding me to his pet this time. He's elected to kill me himself.

Right alongside Bastian Cortez. I can see him clearly now—the bastard lies in a puddle of red liquid that's quickly spreading over the floor. A flickering lightbulb above, illuminates his face—or what remains of the once proud fixer. One of his eyes is swollen shut, and only the harsh planes of his jaw make him recognizable.

"I decided to bring him here," Jaguar continues, returning to my side with a knife raised. It's a deceptively beautiful weapon, made of steel with a handle wrapped in black leather. If Jaguar expects me to tremble at the sight, I don't. I keep my head high and my gaze fixed straight ahead. I won't give him the satisfaction of screaming. I won't…

"Here—" Reaching out, he presses the handle of the blade into my hand. Firm, his fingers curl around mine, helping them find purchase over the leather surface despite my alarm. "I will show you how to hold it."

He manipulates my hand so that I'm extending the knife in front of me. Thick and firm, his fingers nudge mine into the proper position to grasp the short blade. His strong arms encircle me as he does, creating a cocoon as my knees threaten to buckle.

Dripping into my ear, his voice is sinful, coaxing my body into a relaxed state despite every fiber of my being wanting to scream in fear. "You wield it like this," he says, with the same tone he used to coach Franco during their video game sessions. "Keep your grip steady. He'll try to resist you, but his legs are broken. There is nowhere for him to run—"

Wield it. Horror dawns as I realize just what he means. Panicked, I let go of the knife, forcing him to catch it. "I-I don't want to."

"Not this time," he says, moving to stand beside me in a fluid motion. "I won't make you watch, either. But you should know what will happen to any man who threatens you. Who harms you. You are free to go."

He nods toward the door and then steps forward, approaching Bastian, who spits onto the floor at his feet.

"I won't tell you shit," the man says.

"Oh, *sí, sí,*" Jaguar murmurs, crouching down to his level with the knife dangling from his right hand. "You think you won't. For now. But believe me, I can be a very convincing man, as you will soon find out. Lupe—" he inclines his head toward me. "This is your chance to leave."

But I don't. I could blame shock for the sensation that roots me into place, but that's not it. Perhaps curiosity. Diego hurt people in front of me. More than I can count. He wanted to scare me. Horrify me. Traumatize me.

Never once, did he claim the violence was to protect me.

I'm so puzzled by the prospect that, even as Jaguar begins to roll up his sleeves, I don't move. As much as my stomach turns to admit it…the concept of bloodshed as attrition intrigues me. It can't be any different than the horror I've already been exposed to.

Can it?

"Again, Lupe, I am offering you a choice," Jaguar says, his tone uncharacteristically soft. "Make it now."

"I…" *Dios mío*, I barely recognize the voice trickling from my throat. It's too soft. Too calm. "I want to stay."

Jaguar rises, pivoting to face me. "Well then, you have the right to watch," he says. "This is what happens to the men who harm what is mine."

He seems to transform before my eyes, losing any of the softness he displayed before. He's cold, his smile cruel as he gazes down on his prey. God, he looks so much like Gatita that I half expect his canines to lengthen into fangs as he speaks.

"I want answers, you *pendejo*," he growls, turning to kick the huddled Cortez brother in his stomach.

I hear a hiss of pain, and then a grunted, "I'll tell you nothin—"

"There was a woman," I croak, not waiting for Cortez to finish his boast. "A blond. She lured me outside."

"Ah… I remember the one." Jaguar's eyebrows go up in recognition. "Was she working with you?" he growls before issuing another punishing kick to the target of his rage. "Answer me."

A strange feeling floods my body all at once, leaving me dizzy in the aftermath. As Bastian Cortez cowers in Jaguar's shadow, a strange, harrowing thought slams into me—I've had rage directed my way before, but never has it been a weapon utilized at my disposal. No one has ever fought…*for* me. When Bastian spits at his feet, Jaguar doesn't recoil in anger. He throws his head back instead for a laugh I'll hear in my nightmares going forward. It should terrify me.

But it doesn't.

Suddenly Jaguar stills. The absence of his laugh is chilling in the resulting quiet. Only the labored breathing of Cortez can be heard.

"That's okay, *maricón*," he taunts. "Keep your secrets a little longer. You'll be singing like a canary when I'm done. And make no mistake, every fucker involved in your little scheme, man or woman, will be dealt with." Cocking his head, he fixes me with a look that sets my entire body on fire. He manages to convey so much with that single, fiery glance. There isn't a doubt in my mind that he means every word he said.

He won't rest until he has his vengeance—and he won't hoard it selfishly, either. As he clenches his jaw, I sense his intentions, even before he extends his hand toward me in a rare show of deference.

"First, I believe Lupe has some revenge to enact for your violation."

Jaguar faces me fully, and the question in his eyes is clear. Am I ready for this? Do I even want to? Watching the emotions roll across his face is humbling. He doesn't offer this opportunity lightly.

This is a gift that, to him, means more than any purse, or amount of money.

As if sensing my breaking resolve, he slowly inclines his head to that table behind him. Against my own will, my feet start to move, bringing me closer to the long surface cluttered with what I can now see is an array of weapons. Tools.

I reach out, fingering a few implements as I pass them. Another knife. A coil of rope. A hammer, that looks out of place amongst the other sleek, professional devices of torture. Without thinking, I curl my hand around the handle and lift it. Merely to test the weight of it, or so I tell myself. As the dim light glances off the round head, forming the striking surface, I catch my reflection on the metal.

"I like the way you think, Lupe," Jaguar murmurs into my ear. I didn't even see him approach, but this time I lean back as if leeching his strength into my trembling limbs. He feels so damn strong. Impenetrable. Without hesitation, he starts to move, guiding me toward the figure on the floor.

"I think he needs some help, loosening his tongue," Jaguar murmurs into my ear.

Then he crouches, grasping one of the man's meaty arms, forcing his hand flat against the floor.

An invisible switch is flipped in my brain. One second, I'm ready to drop the tool, disgusted by the mere thought of ever using it. But then…

I'm raising it, my eyes on the bastard who gleefully hurt me. As I watch the hammer come down, I stop thinking. Feeling. Caring.

Bang! Bang! Bang!

The sickening series of thuds echo like gunshots as my arms tremble with the force of the impact. Again. Again.

As if from far away, I hear a man's scream as warm liquid sprays over my face. I'm tasting blood, but I can't stop hitting the floor over and over.

"Lupita—" Sternly gentle, Jaguar's voice breaks through my daze as I feel him take the hammer from my grasp. "I think he'll be open to my questions now, chica." His lips press a kiss to my cheek as I realize that I'm on my knees. A whimpering noise reaches my ears, sounding like a whipped animal.

When I eye the man tucked into a fetal position in front of me, I realize what I've done.

"Oh, God—"

"You don't owe him your guilt," Jaguar says, helping me to my feet. "You owe him nothing."

He steps in front of me and stoops to lift the hammer from the floor.

As he lunges toward his prey, I don't flinch away. I watch every last second of how a man like Julian Domingas offers up an apology.

CHAPTER SEVENTEEN

Jaguar once quipped that I look beautiful in red, but he was woefully mistaken. Standing in the master bedroom, casually wiping droplets of scarlet from his cheek, Julian Domingas resembles an avenging angel. A warrior, bathed in bloodshed.

Strangely, he doesn't wallow in the gore, crazy-eyed and ranting like Diego would.

He stands tall. His eyes are crystal clear as he meets the gaze of his own reflection and holds it. He doesn't cringe from the remnants of his violence or brandish them like sparkly adornments.

He is calm and careful as he washes all traces of Bastian Cortez away and, as much as a part of me hates to admit it…

He is so damn beautiful.

"Don't misunderstand what just happened," he says, turning on the faucet to wet his hands. "That wasn't a show put on for your benefit. You heard the bastard yourself."

I did. Unless, Bastian Cortez had been willing to lie until his dying breath, someone else had pulled the strings and made him bold—or desperate—enough to take the risk of kidnapping a woman from under Jaguar's nose.

Should that relieve me?

It doesn't.

"Why do you even care what I think?" I manage to rasp. I'm leaning against the wall just outside the shower, my knees trembling, adrenaline racing through my veins.

"Why?" He shakes his hands dry and turns to face me. Three steps bring him close enough to press his open palm against my cheek. "You expect a man to use you as a toy. A trophy. I have more than enough of those tokens already. I want my woman to understand the world I dwell in and know her place in it. By my side. You can't stand there with your head held high if you doubt my intentions for you. But after tonight… I won't be so understanding if you continue to second-guess me."

A terrifying thought comes to mind. "This is your idea of atonement?" There is no judgment in my voice. As if I were trying to grasp a foreign concept, I sound rather quizzical instead.

"Oh no, chica," he breathes out, his breath hot against my skin. His fingers caress me, running over my forearms in featherlight touches. "This is just the start. An opportunity to brand my idea of loyalty into that beautiful hide. You will never doubt me again."

It doesn't sound like a threat, but something far more sacred. Both a warning and a promise. A statement as obvious as "the sky is blue."

I won't ever doubt him again.

Even if it means more carnage on my behalf. He wasn't the only one drenched in the remains of Bastian Cortez. My hands are red, I realize, looking down.

A sound of disapproval rumbles in the back of Jaguar's throat as he follows my gaze. In a low, rasping tone, he says, "Let me wash you."

In the mirror, I catch a glimpse of myself. As I stand there, stunned, Jaguar begins to strip me of his borrowed shirt.

He's bathed me before, even gently, without that mocking wall he likes to keep up between us. This feels different for a milieu of reasons that go beyond his stern, serious expression. There is a possessiveness in his grip that makes my head swim.

Unlike the last time, he doesn't make me submit to his ministrations. He sits me on a bench built into the wall and crouches between my legs, forcing near-constant contact. His eyes sweep over me with the bold, unashamed nature of a predator taking stock of the territory it's claimed and fought for.

They tell me what he doesn't bother to say out loud—I own this.

When he nears the bruises smarting on my face left by Boaz, a growl erupts from his throat. Real anger in him is nothing like what I'm used to seeing in other men. He doesn't snarl and swagger—only when he's putting on his narco act. The real Julian lets his rage simmer.

"They touched you," he tells me, manipulating a rag and a bottle of soap. "I saw them."

His voice resonates through me, and I can't even formulate a response.

At least until he gruffly commands, "Show me."

I stiffen, my cheeks flaming. "You saw for yourself—"

"I want you to show me." His tone leaves no room for argument. He takes my hand next, manipulating the fingers outward. With his eyes on the trembling digits, he asks, "Where did they hurt you?"

I suck in a breath at the word choice—my own. Shock alone startles me into complying—I point to my thigh, and he guides my hand there, covering it with his own.

"Where else?"

My fingers twitch, moving inward, and he follows, up my inner thigh and then higher.

"Look at me, Lupe."

Our eyes meet at the exact moment that he strokes one of my fingers into extending and then guides it inside me. I cringe at first—it should feel humiliating. The second I start to squeeze my eyes shut in shame, his breath floods my ear, his voice hoarse.

"I claim this," he tells me. "All of this."

With every word, he coxes my own finger even deeper. Held in his grasp, the contact feels different than any other time I might have been driven to touch myself. It's as if his strength leeches into my skin, infecting my muscle and tendons. My own hands take on attributes of his, pairing his firm, unyielding pressure with an unexpected softness.

It feels…

Like heaven and hell in one fell swoop. Like glorious fire and ice. He isn't brutalizing me in this instance—marking me as a dominant predator would. He's making me declare myself as his in a way I can't deny. Can't ignore.

"I want to hear you say it," he grates, his lips against my earlobe. "So, you can imagine yourself saying it to those bastards. You will never need to say these words again. But I want you to engrain them onto your fucking soul, Lupe. I own this."

He urges my finger in deeper. Then almost out. Deeper. Out.

My head rears back against the wall of the stall, and I stare up into the relentlessly falling spray. There is no reason in hell why his words affect me the way they do. I've heard it all before, haven't I? But in the past, those words came with a caveat. I was his...or else. Or else pain. Or else death to myself and those I cared about. I was his—there was no other option.

With Julian, it registers more like a raw, blatant fact. A reality to which there is no alternative. I am his, simply because I am. I need to be. I want to?

"Say it, Lupe," he commands. "Or I will be forced to demonstrate."

My lips flutter apart, but not a word comes out.

"So damn stubborn." He tugs my hand away, and a sense of despair rips through me. It's so strong, I almost cry out. Say something. Don't?

Then his own calloused fingers replace the contact, and I gasp instead. He presses into me with none of the roughness of Bastian Cortez. He isn't brutal, seeking to punish me for letting another man soil what he's deemed as his. He caresses me from the inside out. Makes me melt into his hands. Melt into him.

My cheek meets his shoulder, and all I can do is lace my fingers through his hair and hold on for dear life.

His mouth finds my neck, parting to give way to his raking, nipping teeth. Then he wrenches me from the bench onto his lap, forcing me to clamp my knees around his hips.

I brace for him to enter me himself. Instead, he stands and carries me from the stall, leaving the water running. In a dexterous display of skill, he pivots into the bedroom and lays me on the mattress. I've barely gotten my bearings before his hand hooks beneath my ass, flipping me onto my stomach, facing the opposite end from where he stands.

I groan aloud as his hands fan over my hips and snatch me toward him, angling me until I'm on my knees, but with my front pressed to the mattress. The entire bed shakes as he mounts it after me, and another firm yank draws me directly onto his cock.

My eyelids flutter at the fullness. I grasp at the sheets, fighting for stability as he takes me hard. Punishingly. His hips slam into mine, his nails raking at my skin, his breath like molten fire over the healing marks on my back.

He drives into me with a strength that takes my breath away —this is how he exerts his rage in this instance. Not with pummeling or brutality, but raw, ruthless pleasure. There is no denying the ecstasy. It's sharp, volatile. It makes me writhe as my toes curl helplessly. It makes me bite down on a mouthful of expensive comforter in a pathetic attempt to smother my cries.

It makes me forget everything this man has put me through. Everything this man is capable of.

The way he effortlessly dominates my body… I almost believe him.

"I own this," he growls, running his lips along my spine. "All of this. Say it, Lupe. Tell me with that magic tongue what this magic pussy knew from day one."

It's not fair. My body reacts to his voice, those words, and I don't stand a chance against the resulting firestorm. I feel my eyes roll into my head. My belly quakes. My body grips him like a vice, and he hisses out his approval.

"With that tongue, chica," he demands, his voice thick. "Say it. Fucking say it…"

"You." I clamp my lips against my rebellious tongue, but as my voice echoes off the walls, I don't hear any fear in it. No cowering. No tears or panic. It sounds so damn sure. So confident. That fact alone confuses me so much I lose all control of my senses. "You own this," I tell him.

He slams into me, using the full weight of his body to drive himself home. The resulting pressure acts as a catalyst, triggering a torrent of pleasure that knocks me under. I ride him senselessly, a slave to every ferocious, rocking movement. He takes us across the bed. When I regain my senses, I'm clinging to the edge of the mattress for dear life, seconds from sliding off it headfirst.

Deep down, I know I'll feel the aftermath of this for weeks after. Years, even. When his hand strikes my ass hard enough to sting, he bellows out his own release, and I don't even have enough space left within me to care. To feel regret.

I just wallow in the vicious nature of Julian Domingas, and for a second, I let him have his way. I let us both pretend that I could ever belong to another. I relish in that beautiful lie, and I resist all attempts of the screaming logical part of my brain that tries to tell me otherwise.

I don't know how much time passes when he finally rolls off of me, reaching for something on the nightstand closest to me. I'm too exhausted to pay attention. At least until he drops something onto the bed beside me, in a mass of tangled bedsheets. A book, shiny and brand-new. Hamlet.

"Open it," he commands, sounding as in control as ever.

My heart lurches at the thought of thinking. Reading. I want to lurk in this ignorant, blissed-out mind state forever. It's better than any drug.

But he is persistent. "Open it, Lupe. One of my final tokens of attrition."

Somehow, I force one of my hands to move and flip over the book's lid.

Instead of a fresh, virgin page of text, I find something that makes me lurch upright and scramble back until my shoulder strikes the headboard.

"What is…"

"It is yours," Jaguar says, undeterred by my fear. "Men supply their puppets with purses and shoes. Their *women*? They gift them the means by which they can protect themselves from any harm. The trust that comes with power and peace of mind."

He takes my hand, forcing me to touch the object tucked within a compartment cut into the book itself. The pages have been fused together, creating an ironic, beautiful container for a silver pistol that seems far too small and delicate for him.

I think I knew even before he said it—it's mine.

"Why… Why would you think I want something like this?"

"It isn't about what you want." He makes my fingers curl, lifting the device from its case. "It's what you need. Survival is a gift granted only to the few, Lupe. You will not fear it. You will take it and learn to use it. I will teach you how when you recover."

He takes the gun from me and returns it to its case. Then he sets the fake book on the nightstand, within my reach.

"You would trust me with that?" I croak.

Diego wouldn't have given me a piece of dental floss, convinced I might use it on him. That's the sad part. I never would have. It wasn't until that final night that I even dreamed of hurting him.

"You've held a gun before," Jaguar says, manipulating my body so that I'm lying on my side with my head on the pillows. Then he settles down beside me.

In the seconds that pass next, I don't think I even breathe. Panic roots me to the spot, paralyzing me. "How did you know that?"

"I can see it in you." He captures my hand, holding it above us both. One of his rugged fingers traces my palm, and I shudder at the dangerous taste of friction. "You tense, whenever I touch this finger, right here…" he caresses the knuckle in question. "There is a memory tied to it. One that haunts you still."

I fight my instinct to rip my hand away. "That can't be all."

He laughs, but it's a hollow sound. "It isn't. You cry out in your sleep. Usually, when you've been drugged. Pleading mostly. Sometimes you say, *'I'll do it. I will. Let me go.'* You repeat it until your voice breaks. I've heard such boasts before. I know what context it's usually said in."

I feel so damn violated my body goes limp. Tears prickle my eyes, and there is no holding back. What else did I manage to reveal in such vulnerable moments?

"You killed someone," Jaguar adds, seemingly oblivious to my distress. "*That* I can see in you. There is no mistaking that look. No other source for it." He lowers my hand to the bed and tightens his grip. "I saw it in myself years ago. Perhaps it is cliché, but the first time I killed, I didn't recognize myself due to that look. That faraway gleam in the eye. I quickly learned to suppress it, but you wear it openly, chica. They weren't some random *pendejo*. They mattered to you. Who?"

I close my eyes, triggering more tears to fall.

"I'll let you keep this secret, for now," Jaguar says, and the rasp in his voice makes my heart lurch. It sounds as if he's referring to far more than just one unspoken truth. "I will tell you mine, though. I'm sure you've already put the pieces together yourself. The first man I ever killed was my father. I did so with my bare hands, Lupe, but I didn't plan it. Oh, he was an arrogant man. A real son of a bitch—but he was family. Real men, they do not harm their family. Their blood. They nurture. Shelter. Educate. They are firm, but not cruel. They protect their own, and they do not try to erase ties that go deeper than mere blood."

He says those words with that rare conviction he uses only when it comes to Juan—or when he asked me to carry his child.

"I won't lie to you. I never intended to kill him. I didn't plan it. You, with that magic tongue, were right in at least part of your accusation. It happened when he treated my brother's heart like another pawn in his game. Another way to grow his empire. A toy to give away."

Anger tinges his voice, startling me enough that I open my eyes again. He's staring up at the ceiling, his teeth bared. As if sensing my gaze, his grip on my hand tightens, verging on the point of pain.

"I could have forgiven him for that," he admits in a guttural tone. "Perhaps. But not what he did to the poor bastard he placed Juan's heart into. He molded him, Lupe. Corrected the goodness and purity of my brother. He made him cold. A killer. He made him…"

"Like you," I croak. His twisted logic shouldn't make any sense to me. Nor should I sympathize with a murderer.

But though our body counts most certainty differs, I guess it's fair to say that in that realm, we are the same. Murderers. I have no right to judge him.

"You are the only person in the world I have told that story to," he adds with a low, unsettling laugh. In the same breath, he turns to face me, reaching out to smooth my hair from the space between us. "How does that make you feel, Lupe?"

"I don't know," I admit, sounding broken. "You strike me as the sort of man who isn't frivolous with his secrets. You tell them only to people who you are sure will never use them against you."

"Ah." A corner of his lip quirks in a way that makes my belly flip. "Or I tell my secrets to those with hidden revelations of their own to share. Loyalty is only part of what I want from you. I want what lurks in that skull, chica. I want to know who you killed and why. I want to know the depth of your relationship with the man you cry out for in your sleep. I want to know… Everything."

I can't deny that I'm so damn tempted. Come clean and take whatever punishment he dishes out. For a man who killed his own father for a perceived betrayal, the longer I deceive him about my past, the worse it will be. For all I know, I could wind up in Gatita's cage again the second I let my guard down.

My lips part…

"Not tonight," he says with another rasping laugh. He smooths his hand along my hair, lingering against the back of my skull. "Not while you are broken and shaken. I want you whole when you avail yourself to me. I want to hear that smart fucking mouth at its most spicy. I want you in your right mind when I pick you apart, Lupe. Only then, will you give me what I want."

The request isn't comforting in the slightest. It heralds that patience he has honed so well—the fact that he believes he has all the time in the world to decipher me. To learn me inside and out.

"And when will I get your secrets?" I counter.

Rather than seem annoyed by the impudence, his eyes seem to sparkle. Then he leans in, pressing his mouth to my cheek. There, he murmurs, "I'll feed them to you slowly, Lupe," he says. "Drop by drop, the same way you so greedily took my cock. I wouldn't want you to choke. For now, rest, chica. When you wake, I'll give you the remainder of your gifts. Then you'll cease to look at me with those lost, angry eyes. *Sí?*"

He kisses me again, running his lips over my nose.

"Sleep tight, chica. I'll be here. And if you are worried about what you might say in your sleep…" He draws back enough to meet my gaze, suddenly serious. "You only do so when drugged."

I don't know whether to take that as a threat or a compliment.

CHAPTER EIGHTEEN

I wake up hungry, sore, and exhausted. I don't even want to move, and the persistent pain from my various injuries is bad enough that I almost crave a drug to take the edge off. I am not comfortable in the slightest. These sheets are too soft. The mattress is too decadent. I'm too warm. Too…content.

I hate that I can't blame it on the bed alone. It's the feeling. The warmth that seeps into my skin, undeniably from another body that recently rested beside mine. The smell flooding my nostrils with every breath. A scent that should terrify me—thick, masculine musk.

It lulls me into a dangerous state of mind. One in which I almost forget the danger at my back, and the risk presented by the man this scent belongs to. He'll be the death of me if I let him, in more ways than one. I need to keep my guard up. I need to…

"A contented sigh." The low rasp of approval comes from nearby, and I wrench my eyes open, scanning my surroundings for the source. I find him standing at the foot of the bed wearing only black slacks, his chest bare. Around his neck, he's in the process of draping one of two dark ties he has in either hand. "That must be a good sign. You slept well, Lupe. Good. It's about damn time you enjoyed our bed."

My newfound peace seems to affect my tongue, since a response emerges before I can think it through. "Where…"

Am I? I meant to ask, but it all comes back to me at once— I'm in the master bedroom of some secret mansion in or near California, under the sway of one man.

"You will have me for one more day at least," he says, continuing to test how each of the two ties rests against his bare skin. "Get dressed. I'll have your breakfast brought up to you."

Slowly, I pull myself upright and note that I'm still naked from last night. When I stretch out my limbs, the side beside me still feels warm. He must have only just gotten up.

"My breakfast," I echo. "Is pampering me more of your way of atoning?"

He laughs, and my heart stutters. "No. Oh no, chica. I need you well rested and well fed for what I have in mind for you today."

I grip the sheets beside me so tightly that my nails catch on the delicate fabric. "Oh?" Somehow, I manage to keep the fear from my voice. I think.

His smile widens, and he turns to face me directly. Two steps bring him closer to the bed. Suddenly, he stoops, picking something up from the floor.

"Right on time," he says, eyeing the screen. A muffled sound comes from the device. A cell phone? It's ringing. "Your son is very punctual, Lupe." He hands me the phone, and I look down in confusion.

Then my heart soars, and I rush to answer it.

"Franco! Sweetheart, how have you been?"

"Good!" he chirps. "I like it here. They have lots of games, and I made a friend, Sam. When can you come visit me?"

"Soon, baby," I say hoarsely. I look over to find Jaguar watching me. "Very soon. I miss you so much."

"I miss you too!" He then rushes into a description of his dorm, the grounds, and his eagerness to begin his new courses. He sounds genuinely happy, and the sound of his chatter is enough to wash away any lingering doubts I may have had. Franco couldn't fake this kind of joy.

And I can't deny that only one man has made this possible.

"I have to go to class," he says, startling me back to awareness. "I will call you tonight, okay?"

I smile at the gently stern note in his voice. "Yes, sir. Tonight."

When he hangs up, I sigh and stare at the blank phone screen for so damn long. Finally, I look up. Jaguar has settled on a tie, it seems. He's pulling on a black dress shirt over his tattooed chest, and my heart skips another beat. I rack my brain but can't remember a time he wore formal clothing.

Just what does he have in store?

"I told him he should make time for his mama in the morning before class, and in the evening before bed. It seems he doesn't need much encouragement to do so," Jaguar explains, examining the cuffs of his sleeves. "Ruthless ambition must run in the family."

I picture Tiena and cringe. He doesn't even know half of it. Still, I can't deny that he didn't have to help Franco at all.

"Thank you," I croak. "For doing that. It's good to hear that he's okay."

"If we are to return in time for you to speak to him later, we should leave soon." He fishes a cell phone from his pants pocket and utters a terse command I don't catch. Then he turns to me and sheds his shirt, draping it over the end of the bed.

"It seems you don't share the same enthusiasm for morning as Francisco," he says.

I hold my breath as he advances and lifts me into his arms as though I weigh nothing. My hands instinctively lace together around his neck and before I can stop myself, I have my head resting on his shoulder. Without a word, he carries me into the en suite and commences with what I'm starting to realize must be a task he enjoys—bathing me from head to toe. He works slowly and carefully as if branding all traces of him into my skin.

When he's satisfied, he bundles me in a towel and makes me sit on the edge of the bed while he dries my hair and arranges the damp strands loosely around my face. Our breakfast has arrived, and he watches me eat woodenly from a tray of food I assume has been meticulously prepared by Horatio. As I swallow down the last bites, Jaguar enters the closet and returns seconds later with a black dress exquisitely cut and probably worth more than anything I've worn in my entire life.

As he helps me into it, I notice that it's starkly different from the flashy designs his harem women wear. It wasn't picked out blindly without care given to the body that might wind up wearing it. This was designed with my shape in mind. My curves or lack thereof. He chose it for me.

"Beautiful," he declares when I'm dressed. A pair of heels complete the look, and he hands me the purse I found waiting for me the other day and my new cell phone. "Let's go."

We leave the house, flanked by two of the guards he brought with him, but a fancy car isn't waiting for us out front. Instead, Jaguar leads us down a path toward a garage large enough to hold at least four different vehicles. His preferred SUV is there, as well as a couple fancy sports cars, and a luxury sedan.

"Having trouble deciding which of your toys to take out today?" I quip, surprising myself. The man beside me has put me through an emotional and psychological roller coaster more times than I can count. It should be impossible to return to our twisted dynamic so easily.

Maybe I've grown soft in the years after Diego, so desperate to convince myself that I'm not that weak woman anymore. I won't be fooled again or fall prey to the next man to show an interest.

The sad part is that it would be easy to write off Jaguar as another clone of my vicious ex. Too easy. But a part of me suspects that a man as cunning as he is has far more means in mind to trap his lovers than violence and brutality.

He uses charm.

"No," he says against my ear, wrapping an arm around my waist. "You get to pick today. Choose carefully, Lupe. I know you can drive. If you could take out any of these 'toys,' which would it be?"

I suck in a breath and release it in a nervous laugh. "Well, I think I would pick that one." I point to the flashiest of the two sports cars in a bright shade of cherry red. "Would you be worried I'd scratch it?"

"No." He presses something into my hand that I glance down to inspect—and nearly choke.

"It's yours," he says.

My face heats though I manage to force out a smile to swivel to face him. "These keys don't look like the ones I found yesterday. Did you change your mind about which of these toys to give me?"

He chuckles and moves past me to claim the driver's side of my chosen car. Meeting my gaze, he says, "The key I gave you was to the garage itself." He gestures to the spacious room itself. "They are *all* yours, chica. Get in."

I feel my eyes widen. I have to blink several times and force myself to climb into the passenger seat.

"You seem stunned," Jaguar remarks. "Don't tell me you doubt the gesture."

Do I even believe him? I'm too terrified to tell.

"I'm just wondering how I'm going to fit all this into my luggage when you send me back to Texas."

"Oh, Lupe, you can drive them back to Texas if you wish. With me by your side."

"Where are we going?" I ask, rather than try to dissect the nuances of that statement.

He cocks his head and eyes the road. "I think it's time you had a day out on the town. Only, unlike Franco, I will pick the places we go. *Claro?*"

I hold my breath, too uneasy to respond. Where could a man like Julian Domingas take someone with the so-called purpose of having a good time? The possibilities are chilling.

"Don't look so worried, chica," he says. "We just need to get something out of the way first. Then I think you will enjoy our destination."

If he's aiming to comfort me, he doesn't.

Not in the slightest.

Despite knowing Jaguar's penchant for the unpredictable, I don't think I would have ever guessed where he'd take me—a shooting range.

It's open air, in the middle of nowhere, with human-shaped targets spaced at various distances from a shooting line.

Without my knowledge, he brought along the pistol he bought me or one suspiciously like it. Gently, he shows me how to hold it properly, forced to lean over me in the process. I bite my lip at the reaction coursing through me. He's so damn warm. So firm. My mind starts to wander, envisioning if the growing pressure I feel against my lower back is another weapon he has holstered at his front, or something else…

"Focus, Lupe," he chides, his tone a dangerous mix of playful and stern. "Watch." With unnerving patience, he shows me where to place my fingers and how to brace my weight against the kickback. How to operate the weapon. Clean it.

And how to aim.

"I don't give a damn if you're outnumbered or bleeding out. First, you take a breath. Then face your enemy. Look them in the eye if you can. As a woman, they will always underestimate you, and right when they open their mouths to tell you some sexy little threat. You—" He makes me squeeze the trigger, and a shot rings out. Instantaneously, a small hole appears in one of the targets, mere centimeters from the bullseye.

"You don't hesitate," he murmurs into my ear. "You don't cower. You don't flinch in fear." He steps aside and leaves me holding the gun alone.

"Again. Let's see if you have magic aim in addition to that magic tongue."

I suck in a breath and aim at the next target, following Jaguar's advice to the letter. The night when I shot Diego, I had no clue of what to do other than pull the trigger. I was frightened. Shaking. I think I fired at least four times but hit him only once in a spray of blood that rendered him silent. It wasn't clean. It wasn't brave.

It wasn't easy.

"Don't forget the most important step, Lupe," Jaguar warns. "No hesitation."

I fire and come the closest to the bullseye I have since starting.

Jaguar claps, his playful smirk on display. "Excellent. I'll make a fighter out of you yet. Now, let's go. Business is over. It's time for play."

He takes the gun and stows it somewhere unseen. Then we return to the car and arrive at another destination minutes later. This one, however, makes my heart trill in a way that has nothing to do with reliving past gun violence.

"Ah, this is what I love to see," Jaguar murmurs, his eyes on my face. "The look when the cat has got your tongue, chica, and you forget to maintain that hard-ass mask. If I'm not mistaken, one might assume that I've pleased you." He reaches out, running his thumb along my cheek in a gentle caress.

I bite my tongue, holding my judgment until we're inside.

Once we are, I can't contain my awe anymore.

"I know you are one for grand gestures, but I didn't think irony was your forte. Your other women wish for shopping sprees and fun. You bring me to a library."

"A bookstore," he clarifies with an unsettling laugh. "We are here to source items for your new library, Lupe. After that, we can call ourselves, as they say, 'even.'"

"Even," I croak.

Who could have guessed that a narco's idea of making up for a mistake would be to source his lover a private library? A part of me still expects a catch to come. Some caveat to add a dangerous twist to the request.

As Jaguar leads me through a grand, elegant lower level and up a flight of stairs, I think I've found it. Once inside an upper room, it becomes clear that Jaguar didn't intend for me to have free rein of the entire store. He had a selection curated and arranged in a room that must be reserved for book signings or other gatherings.

An impressive arrangement of leatherbound books with golden filigree titles is arranged on a large oak table. I finger one and try my damn hardest to contain my reaction. Still, I'm sure my voice breaks as I read aloud, "The Complete works of Shakespeare. Impressive, Jaguar. I didn't take you as a collector."

Especially when he seems to treat women and allies like disposable commodities as easily switched out as a pair of shoes.

"They aren't mine," he says. "Yours, if they suit that haughty little taste of yours. Pick what you want. Price is no option."

I swallow hard, both thrilled and terrified by the prospect.

I turn away and eye the books on the shelves in this room. Something tells me that his directive extends beyond it, to the entire store.

And, damn it, any shred of a grudge I've fought to maintain shrivels and crumbles away. I'm not stupid, though. I know that a man like him is dangerous to trust. Lethal to underestimate. If I let my guard down around him too much, I won't ever see the knife he decides to embed in my back.

"And what if I said that I wanted them all?" I laugh, amused by my own boast.

But he doesn't join in. Suddenly stern, he approaches me and captures my chin against his palm. "I would say… Don't wish for things you don't truly want. My woman asks, and she receives. I told you that before. So, if you want the whole damn store, say that you want the whole damn store. Don't play coy with me."

I suck in a breath, caught off guard by the intensity in his voice. When his fingers flex impatiently against my skin, I choke out, "I don't. I just want… I want you to read to me. Like I wanted before. Do you remember?"

His lips twist into a devastating smile. "Oh, I remember, chica. In fact, I picked out a book already I could read to you. Care to hear?"

I approach the desk and run my fingers along the polished surface, desperate to hide how they shake. "Oh?"

True to his word, he must have planned out his moment in his head, down to exactly what I'd ask for. He slides the text in question from the desk, angling the cover so that I can't see it, and moves to sit in a leather armchair. Patting his knee, he cocks his head in my direction. "Sit."

My belly flips over as I inch toward him on trembling legs. When I come close enough, he wrenches me down and settles one of his hands over my waist while flipping the book open with the other. With his lips near my ear, he begins to read.

And with every word, a chilling mixture of shock and excitement run down my spine.

He upheld my request from days ago when I begged him to read his favorite quotes to me. He does so while wrapped within the original text, leaving only the raspiness of his baritone to tell which words mean the most to him.

"…In the end, it is impossible not to become what others believe you are."

I lean against him, mulling over those words and the guttural way in which he said them. They weren't an idle quote, picked at random from the play *Julius Caesar*. Much like the first time he quoted this particular work to me, I sense there is a riddle laced within every word.

The world claims that he is a monster, and I think he is more than capable of living up to that descriptor and more. He isn't ashamed of the role he's had to take on. If anything, he seems to excel at playing the part perfectly.

So yes, his quote means far more than it appears to on the surface. He isn't referring to himself.

"Tell me, what am I, Julian?" I ask him outright, contorting my neck to better see his face.

Those eyes gleam, pleased I solved his riddle—or perhaps pleased that I forged yet another pathway of intimacy between us. "You, Lupita…" He slides his hand toward my inner thigh. "You are an interesting woman to decipher. Bold one minute. Shattered the next. Cunning. Too damn smart for your own good. The woman who prizes loyalty and honesty above all. Yet, she constantly lies."

I stiffen. "About what?"

"The man who has you," he says, catching me off guard. "You've claimed that it could be me, but I don't know if I believe you, Lupe. I think I need to hear you say it."

I run my tongue over my suddenly dry lips. "Say?"

"Don't be coy." He grabs my chin, forcing me to look directly into his eyes. "I want to hear you say that I have you. All of you. In that sexy little moan you make when you think I'm not paying attention. When you think hard fucking is all I want."

His lips find my ear again, and all I can do is stare at the nearest bookshelf as he hums his next words directly into it.

"I've seen you. Even this morning. When I'm so deep inside you, you can't think of anything else. You can't block me out."

He wrenches me around, so I have to straddle him, and our foreheads meet, his eyes on my mouth.

"Tell me that I'm the only man you want. That I have you. Say it."

I know better than to hesitate. "You have me—"

"No," he snarls. "Not like that."

His hand worms beneath my skirt and finds the rim of my panties. My breath catches, and a realistic fear creeps into my brain, making me justify trying to climb off him.

"What if someone comes in—"

"They won't." He yanks me onto him and laces his fingers together behind my back, trapping me. His tone alludes to the very real possibility that he informed any employees that we aren't to be disturbed, hence the private room well above the sales floor.

"Sound travels, Jaguar," I say, fighting to sound playful. "You really want to hear me scream for you here?"

"No," he admits, his eyes unreadable. "But I want to see which of your true loves wins out. You think I didn't catch the greedy way you eyed my library, Lupe? Oh, it's a look I recognize. Hunger. A thirst for knowledge in the way most women look at pretty dresses and priceless shoes. It's the way more women look at me. Greedy. Not you. You're eager for the secrets in my head, but you don't want any more than that. You've lied to yourself more than to me, I think. Convinced yourself that you can fake it enough. Lie to us both enough. Maybe one day you'll believe it. Make no mistake. I didn't bring you here to pamper you or woo you. I'm not entirely aiming to coddle you after what happened with those bastards, either. Money alone could do that. No. I want something more than your gratitude. I want to see that gleam in your eye."

He goes silent, daring me to ask.

"What gleam?"

A smile shapes his lips, but it's a mocking caricature of the expression.

"The one you had when you jumped off a two-story balcony and into my pool, Lupe. When you shouted at me to reveal your lover and parade him before you. Remember that?"

My throat goes dry. "That was fear."

"Keep telling yourself that," he says coldly. "In any case, I don't want an echo of what you harbor for another man. I want that fantasy you had, remember?"

He runs his hand through my hair, disturbingly gentle. "You pretended as though you'd fucked Braulio like that, but it was a lie, wasn't it? No, you dug deep for that one, Lupe. I want to know what you were thinking about?"

Damn him. It never ceases to amaze and terrify me just how perceptive a man he is. Yet, cunning enough to play along with my act only to reveal the truth later when I least expect it. A part of me warns that he's seen through far more than what he's led on. Why not ask him?

"You tell me, *Julian*," I say, fighting to keep my voice steady. Our breaths mingle, and from this angle, I have a clear view into those dangerous eyes and his chilling thought process.

"Fine. You were thinking of a man that wasn't either myself or your Braulio. One you dreamt up, I think. I recognized that far-off look in your eye. The way you relaxed into me. You weren't reliving a memory, I'm sure of that. You were making one up."

My face heats. "I think you overestimate my imagination—"

"Oh, but I haven't." His grip on my waist lowers until he's palming my ass in both hands, kneading the globes of muscle. "If anything, I think I may have underestimated the lengths you'd go to endure the task you've set up for yourself. You aim to keep me sweet on you, Lupe. But, at the same time, you are driven to keep as much of a wedge between us as you can. Before, I thought it was because you were still working with him. Your lover. That he had a little leash around that pretty neck. I've since changed my mind."

"Oh?" I croak.

"I've come to understand that you don't even realize you're doing it—closing yourself off from me. It comes as naturally to you as a viper flashing its fangs when threatened. That is what makes you so dangerous, chica." He strokes his thumb along my chin. "You rely on instinct. Reckless impulse. You are the kind of woman who decides whether she can love a man or not in an instant. But trust? That can take years to earn, no matter how willing you seem to give it. My Gatita was the same way."

"Is comparing me to your pet your idea of a compliment?"

He laughs. "She is not a pet. She would kill me in a heartbeat if I gave her a chance. I would never put it past her. The same way I don't doubt that you could turn that gun on me the second you thought me a threat. I can see you wrestling with the decision to stay or flee every fucking second. It's endearing, for now. You want so badly for me to trust you."

"And do you?"

It's a dangerous question to ask a man like him. I don't do so lightly. I hold my breath as I watch the gears in his brain turn in painfully slow motion. Finally, his smile widens.

"Perhaps I do. You'd learn the second I don't. But we can save those messy topics for another conversation, chica. For now, I want you to repay the favor I have bestowed."

My heart skips a beat. Does he mean buy him a garage filled with luxury cars? No. His request is far more nuanced than that.

"Whisper your favorite quote into my ear," he murmurs. "I want to know what words a sexy viper-kitty lives by."

"I don't have one—"

"Liar," he scolds. "You do so without even realizing it, Lupe. That faraway look always betrays you."

I open my mouth to deny it—then I realize… He's right. Perhaps there is one quote I've lived by, but for so long that I've forgotten where it came from. Ironically, he must be partial to the same phrase because he's used it in front of me.

"Men are masters of their own fate."

"That's not what I asked for," he murmurs.

I bite my lip before leaning forward, brushing my lips along his ear lobe. Low and raspy, I repeat the quote.

And a sound rumbles from his throat that I have never heard. Thickened. Guttural. Violent.

"Again."

"M-Men are—"

His hands ghost between my legs. What feels like a thumb hooks beneath the rim of my panties, sliding against the uncovered flesh, and my breath catches.

"Lupe," he warns, and I race to voice the words again.

Pleased, he shoves two fingers inside me at once, and I feel my eyes roll back into my skull.

"And who is the master of you?" he wonders, his voice alarmingly deep.

Damn him. If this were some sexy, romantic play, I would know the line I'm meant to say. *You, Jaguar. You are my master.* Somewhere in the middle of enduring his touch, a new answer springs to my lips before I can hold it back.

"Me."

He chuckles. Thankfully, I don't sense anger in the sound. Just… Amusement? Pleasure.

"Ah, there is an honest answer," he says, his voice grated with praise. "You keep that mind under lock and key, but I think you could enjoy relinquishing some control to me."

"For what?" I find myself gasping in response.

He slides those fingers deeper inside me, twisting them in ways that make me gasp for air and writhe on his lap like a woman possessed. It's cruel how he does it—simulating the ease with which a puppet master controls his doll.

"Because I can show you that world you've dreamt about but never thought you'd taste for yourself," he says. "You know the one. The power and control you've lusted after for so damn long, all while convincing yourself that you didn't care for it."

I don't like how convincing he can sound. As if he believes it. As if it's true.

Rather than challenge him outright, I point out the glaring flaw in his logic. The one thing that the actions of him and other men have taught me over and over again.

"Men like you never share their power."

"Perhaps," he admits while tilting his head so that I'm facing him again. The next second, his tongue slides along my lower lip, urging both apart. "But we can gift it to those deemed worthy enough. Is that woman you?"

I feel myself relax into him, tentatively brushing his tongue with mine.

"Perhaps," I say, copying his use of the word. "But nothing I say will change your mind. You've already made it up. It's why you had me jump through so many hoops. You aren't a man who decides things lightly."

A facet of his personality that I've learned the hard way. The man is a convoluted puzzle, changing his methodology at every turn. Never once do I feel as though I have him entirely deciphered.

He doesn't respond, instead issuing one of those unsettling, calculating laughs.

This close to him, I'm more tempted than ever to push his buttons and gauge his reaction. It's either that or relinquish myself to the overwhelming sexuality he exudes without even trying.

So, I position his earlobe between my teeth and bite down. Not hard, just enough to cement the sting of my next words.

"I don't want your empire, Julian," I tell him. "I'm more than content with this kind of power."

I reach between us and undo his fly, freeing his cock in seconds. A rasping grunt resonates through his chest as I take him into my hand. My thoughts race with fears of a poor oblivious salesclerk stumbling in, but I'm willing to trust him in this instance. So, I guide him inside me and quiet the building hunger simmering in my body for now.

Even he can't accuse me of lying about this—I love riding him. It provides a vantage point of him unlike any other. I can feel his heartbeat raging against mine. Taste the heat of his breath. Hear him groan with every inch I take.

For several agonizing seconds, he lets me pretend to hold the reins. Then he grips my waist and snatches me into him.

The forceful friction compared with the depth he can achieve, takes my breath away. I groan through clenched teeth, fisting handfuls of his hair. The leather chair conforms to our combined weight, and I feel like we're suspended in some twisted version of heaven where the devil reigns supreme. He has me by the throat, and I'm willing to see just where this latest sin will lead.

Though at the back of my mind, I know that I'm in danger of losing far more than just my proverbial soul.

He presses his lips to mine with a gentleness I don't expect. Then he pulls back and changes tact. Before I can think to react, his teeth are raking the flesh of my throat between them.

"You are mine, Lupita," he growls, sealing his claim with a harder bite. "Say it."

A moan escapes my lips instead, but he won't let me evade his command that easily.

CHAPTER NINETEEN

When the heady, after-sex glow wears off, he helps me climb from his lap. I expect him to whisk us from the store next, but he surprises me yet again.

"You haven't made your selections," he says with dead seriousness. "Surprise me, Lupe. Pick both your favorites and the topics a sexy viper-kitty is eager to learn."

I take him up on that offer and spend what feels like hours gathering a sizeable collection of volumes. Where he'll put them? I have no idea. Perhaps he'll burn them before me in the name of yet another test.

This man is so damn unrelenting in the mystery he likes to present to the outside world. Just when I think I have him figured out, he turns the tables.

Like now.

"You seem shocked, Lupe," he murmurs into my ear as we return to the house and find an army of movers out front, steadily carrying boxes upon boxes inside.

He delights in my confusion, I think. He loves to catch me off guard, and I try to put on a good show of being unmoved.

But there is no mystery to unravel this time. The objects the movers heft between them are simple enough to make out. Bookshelves. A lot of them, plenty to stock my own private library.

But they aren't the only new arrival. I can sense a change even before Jaguar remarks, "We will have guests arriving tonight, but we will discuss that later."

"Guests?" My heart sinks. I hate the crippling, paralyzing fear that creeps over me next, but I can't resist it. How this man loves to unnerve me right when I think I have him sussed. He's already devised yet another game.

"You aren't the one in the cooking pot this time, Lupe," he says with an uncharacteristic bit of warmth in his voice. Gently, he cradles my chin against his palm, and I almost feel reassured by the gesture. Almost. "You will merely help to put my prey on edge, though you will not understand without some backstory. Backstory I'm not in the mood to give just yet. Come."

He cuts a path through the wandering workmen and leads me upstairs to his room. Our room. If I didn't believe that before, he's taken great pains to drive that point home.

I gape at the subtle but effective changes to the design that make his intentions apparent—even more so than earlier. There are bags strewn over the floor, with partially unpacked mementos all over. His. These are the personal effects he kept hidden from view at his main villa. His books, all tattered with use. His clothing.

"Do you remember the story I told you?" he asks, coming up behind me, hooking his arm around my waist. "About my father?"

I nod. "Yes." My heart clenches with foreboding. Is this his prelude to yet another mind game at my expense?

As if sensing my train of thought, he cups my chin with his palm, forcing me to meet his gaze directly. "And?"

"And Juan," I add. "What happened to him."

"And Navid?" His voice dips into a disarming, gruff rumble. Whirling around, I inspect his expression and shudder. He's angry again, but I suspect this wrath isn't meant for me.

"Yes," I croak. "The boy your father chose as Juan's recipient—"

"Chose," he says with a cold chuckle. "I think I prefer that word choice. When my father *chose* Navid to replace his true son, well he initiated him into the Domingas family— whether the bastard wanted to be or not. Our family rises to the occasion when one of us is threatened."

"Is he who you plan on arriving?" I ask cautiously. This topic still feels like a landmine. I can't even imagine what type of man this Domino must be. Someone even Jaguar refers to with a twisted mixture of resentment but maybe a little respect as well?

"The men who have Pedro are not the average *pendejos*," Jaguar admits. "They are skilled. Clever. Even I can admit that. It will take more than some random, untrained bastard to track them down."

"But you will?" I ask. "Hunt him down. Please, I'll do anything you ask."

Or, the first chance I get, I'll leave this place and hunt Pedro down myself.

"You don't need to beg for my assistance," Jaguar snaps. His hand captures my chin, forcing me to meet his probing stare. The anger I find in those dark eyes surprises me. This time, I'm the source of it. "I thought I made that clear. You've earned the right to command my help. So, demand it. My woman will never beg any man. Not even me."

I shudder at the implication of that statement. Facets of it feel way too dangerous to dwell on now. My status with Jaguar can wait. For now, Pedro and Franco's safety are all that matter.

"Help me find him. I won't leave him with those monsters. I can't."

He smiles as he releases me. "You don't even realize the concessions I've made for you already. My men are on it, but getting close to the bastards won't be easy. Which is why I need you to tell me everything you know about your old lover."

I'm holding my breath without realizing it. When I breathe again, I'm aware of him watching me like a hawk. Tentatively, I say, "You know about him." I can't even bring myself to say his name. After days in Jaguar's thrall, maybe I wanted his possessive lust to drive Diego from my mind for good.

"I've known from the start that your lover was never Braulio," Jaguar says evasively. "A woman like you? Ah, you would have smothered that bastard in his sleep. You try to hide it, but that viper spirit is evident to any man who likes his women feisty. You were never Braulio's."

"And I'm sure a man with your resources already did research into me. Who I really am."

"Who you are doesn't mean shit to me," Jaguar says with a dismissive shrug. "It never did. I only place stock in what I can see and verify for myself. You claimed to be Franco's mother, and you've acted as such from the start. Your name. Your identity. It was always trivial. But yes, Lupita, I've known who you are for a while now."

"So why the games?"

"Why not? I like to know the mettle of my opponents. Where their loyalties truly lie."

"And you know about Diego," I say hoarsely. "For how long?"

"Since the night you dove into my pool from a second-story window," he says. "Did you really think I wouldn't question that level of desperation? I know Braulio. You wouldn't fear that bastard half as much. Only a true monster could have you so shaken."

"And yet, you think I loved him."

"Wrong," he scolds. "I know you do. I may not be well versed in the emotion, Lupe, but I can tell when a man has the interest of a woman. I can see him in you. You even cry for him some nights. Did you know that?"

"I don't… I hate him," I say thickly. "I never long for him. Never."

"Tell yourself that if you must," Jaguar says. "For now, we will focus on Pedro. To find him, I can't rely on my usual men. Your Diego is a smart bastard. He's evaded all of my attempts to track him down. In fact, it was only recently that I settled on his identity at all."

"How?"

"Your concern for Francisco," he says. "It was no secret Tiena Sanchez didn't give a fuck about her son. But why take on her identity in the first place? I knew the answer lay in your past. You were afraid of someone."

"So, was this all just an elaborate ruse to get me to open up to you?"

A darkness falls over his expression. "Don't make any mistake, Lupe. You weren't honest with me from the start, but I have been nothing but clear about my intentions for you—" He strokes my cheek in a chilling caress. "You are mine—do you hear me? I knew from the second you sauntered up to me with those gleaming, secretive eyes that

I would have you. Me. I won't surrender my prize to another man. You made your choice when you promised yourself to me. I will take what I am owed."

My mind reels. Does he really mean that? God, I can't tell. His voice sounded emphatic enough to make me shudder with apprehension.

"And if I decide that I don't want to be owned by any man?"

He chuckles, and his upper lip quirks into a smirk. "That is what I like about you, my Lupe. That curiosity. It's sexy as hell, especially when you already know the answer to your question. Leave me if you want. Test my patience. We will have a hell of a time, you and I. And, after I've punished you for your insolence, you might even enjoy the makeup sex."

I can't breathe. All I can do is fight for air and try to stay standing.

"How does Navid factor into all of this?" I demand, turning back to the topic at hand. "Finding Pedro."

His expression falls. "As much as it pains me to admit, Navid is a competent tracker. He goes by Domino now, and the bastard is under the radar. I doubt your Diego will expect me to utilize him. Our relationship is strained, one could say. No one would expect he could ever work for me willingly."

"And why would he? If he hates you."

"Because you are going to convince him to," Jaguar says. "Navid can deny me at the point of death. But you? You and that magic tongue will be able to convince him in a way that I can't. He never could shy from the chance to be a hero."

"You said he's under the radar. Why? How do you know where to even find him?"

"Let's just say I have my ways," he says. "He should be here by tonight. And you…" He strokes the hair from my face. "You will be tasked with making sure I don't kill the motherfucker."

Oddly enough, I'm not put off by the casual mention of violence. This is how Julian Domingas operates—in a constantly shifting game of pros and cons. For once, he's letting me see his thinking process up close, and I can't deny that I'm intrigued.

"Tell me about him," I demand.

He beckons me closer with a nod of his chin and sits, settling me onto his lap. "What do you want to know."

"Who is he? Navid?"

"A selfish bastard unworthy of the Domingas name, and yet… He is family. He has experience working as a double agent, feeding the cartel info on our closest rivals. Up until recently, he worked for a man by the name of Roy Pavalos."

"Let me guess. You were behind that chaos."

He smirks. "You don't seem very surprised, Lupe. How else would I build my empire? By kissing babies and holding hands?"

"No," I admit. "It's just... If you hate this man so much, why keep him alive? Especially if he betrayed you once."

His eyes narrow. I've struck too close to the truth. Will he reveal yet another piece of himself to me, or shut down?

I reach out for his hand, suddenly eager for him to pick the first option. I'm already drunk on the snippets of Julian Domingas he's fed me. I want more. I crave it.

"I want to know," I say, testing out his previous request. He wants me as his willing partner? Well then, partners are allowed to make demands of each other, are they not?

I hunt his eyes as they process my request, glittering with mystery. Suddenly, he thumbs my lower lip, making both part beneath the pressure. "Domino is a capable bastard. You tell me why I might want to keep his lying, traitorous ass around."

"Because... At the end of the day, he still has a part of Juan alive inside him," I say, my eyes widening at the revelation. "He is still your brother, whether you want him to be or not."

He doesn't react to the statement, but I sense it's the cold, bitter truth—and it's yet another subtle warning to me. Should I ever be insane enough to bear a child for this man, that will cement an unbreakable tie between us. He will never let me go.

"Ah, I know that look," he scolds, stroking my chin. "That shocked, fearful expression as though I pulled out a knife and pressed it to your throat. Tell me why that is."

It's my turn to bare a part of myself to him. Am I ready to do so? Hell no. My heart feels so heavy in my chest. The weight drags my body down until he's fully supporting me. The scary part? He does so without question.

"I don't know if I can let myself be owned by you," I confess.

He doesn't react, at least not outwardly—but I feel his hand tighten its grip on my ass, a subtle reminder of his hold over me.

"And why is that? After all, you came to me, promising me your heart and soul."

"It's one thing to be a trophy," I say. "It's another to be… Consumed."

Wholly, without question.

I can't tell what he's thinking behind those dark, fathomless eyes. When his upper lip quirks into a smirk, there is no warmth in it.

"I've had women as trophies," he says. "I keep them on a pedestal. I keep them sweet and dressed in whatever designer bullshit they desire. I keep them at arm's length, and I prefer it that way. From day one, you challenged that. You wormed your way into my inner circle with a skill I must admit I found charming, at first… You claim you don't want to be owned, but that's what your body screams for when I'm buried inside of you. Me. Me alone. No one else."

I fight to suck in air, dizzy by the imagery he paints in such a dangerous, lethal tone.

"And why is that so different from the others?" I ask. "They all want you. They'd give their souls to have you claim them. Keep them. Why am I any more appealing than them?"

"Ah, you hit the nail on the head," he says. "They want me. The money. The power. But what is it you want, Lupe? You claim to be after the materialistic, but there's more to it than that. You crave protection. Stability. That is what I can give you, and yet you turn your nose up at my attempts. You aren't as easy to please as a bitch who wants a nice purse and new shoes. You present a challenge, and I don't walk away from those so easily."

"Oh?" I snipe back. "You had no problem entertaining your trophies back in Texas."

Irrational anger burns through me at the mental image of those bitches fighting to climb onto his lap or laid out in the bed next to him.

"You caught that, did you," he replies, an eyebrow raised. "I was wondering why you would let another touch what is yours without repercussions. If you must know... I haven't fucked another since that magic pussy claimed me."

I suck in a breath at the confession. A man as virile as him, supposedly restraining himself for me alone? The thought makes me reckless enough to play along with his devious fantasy.

"So, if I give in to you," I begin, my voice husky. "If I let you make me a part of your family, will you then lose interest? Will another fiery chica with a magic pussy be enough to make you stray?"

"Maybe," he says. His honesty is both blunt and oddly refreshing. I'm so sick of being toyed with and manipulated. This is how he really operates—a never-ending game of chess. "But my woman? She would combat any threat to her kingdom with violence. I pity the woman who would try to take what is hers."

"And you? If I found another man to—"

Suddenly his expression shifts. This isn't a game anymore. We've crossed a line into uncharted territory, and I am woefully unmatched. Lust is what I know. Not love, and certainly not the limits of a healthy relationship.

"I'd gut him in front of you," Jaguar promises in a beautiful murmur. "Slowly. I'd make you watch every cut. Every drop of blood spilled. I'd make you savor every one of his screams and cries. No one will ever take what is *mine*."

Rather than alarm me, the boast sends a thrill down my spine. Excitement? I picture Diego at the mercy of his knife the way Bastian Cortez was. Do I enjoy that prospect? My heart lurches in a way I'm willing to interpret as a yes.

"Oh, I can see that you're beginning to understand," Jaguar says, his voice a heart-stopping rasp. "My woman, so fucking bloodthirsty. Tell me who you need me to kill."

His eyes glow with unrestrained hunger. Could I really be capable of destroying Diego once and for all? Maybe.

Licking my lips, I suck in a breath. "I want—"

"*Jefe!*"

Suddenly a commotion comes from below. I hear Horatio shout something I can't decipher.

I lurch upright. Oh, God. Diego?

Jaguar, however, hasn't budged. With an almost bored expression, he sighs. "Domino has arrived."

CHAPTER TWENTY

Jaguar leads the way from the room without answering the multitude of questions I levy at his back. We're halfway down the staircase when I note shifts in the atmosphere that have nothing to do with the movers still dutifully performing their tasks.

Tension gathers in Jaguar's muscles, radiating off him in waves. Suddenly he stops and reaches out for me. With our fingers entwined, we descend the remaining stairs. At the foot of the stairs already waits Horatio, his expression grim.

"They are here," he says.

Domino Valenciaga. Despite his obvious hatred, Jaguar seems to think he is the only one capable of helping us rescue Pedro, but I sense there is more to his past with Domino than he's let on.

Can I trust this new player in our game?

It looks like I don't have long to decide. Behind Horatio stand two strangers, lingering in the foyer.

One is a small woman, breathtakingly beautiful. Towering over her is a slender man with watchful eyes.

"Alright, you son of a bitch," he growls, curling his hands into fists. "What do you want now?"

~ Continue Jaguar and Lupita's story in Blood Brothers ~

A WORD FROM THE AUTHOR

Hey there!

Thank you so much for reading! If you enjoyed the story, please leave a review and recommend the book to any friend you think would love this twisted world. You'd have my eternal gratitude. Even a short sentence goes a long way!

Then, come join the rest of us dark romance lovers in my Facebook Group where you can get snippets, sneak peeks of upcoming books and even help vote on aspects of future novels.

Come to the dark side:
https://www.facebook.com/groups/lanasbeautifulmonsters/

WANT MORE STUFF TO READ?
Join my newsletter and get a **free book**! Plus, you get to stay updated with any new releases, random giveaways and exclusive sneak peeks!
https://www.lanaskybooks.com/newsletter

Other Novels: https://lanaskybooks.com/

ABOUT THE AUTHOR

Lana Sky is a reclusive writer in the United States who spends most of her time daydreaming about complex male characters and parenting her Cockapoo Joey. She writes dark, twisted romance across several genres. Her titles include everything from mafia romance to vampires.

facebook.com/AuthorLanaSky

twitter.com/lanasky101

amazon.com/author/lanasky

pinterest.com/lanasky101

goodreads.com/lanasky

instagram.com/lanasky101

bookbub.com/authors/lana-sky

tiktok.com/@author_lana_sky

www.ingramcontent.com/pod-product-compliance
Lightning Source LLC
Chambersburg PA
CBHW072026220726
48293CB00016B/449